In this tale you will meet all your favourite fairy tale characters, both old and new, who assist Jack in his endeavors to succeed in the realm of imagination. All who live in this book reside in a world of magic and fantasy.

The Twisted Tale of Jack and The Beanstalk is the story of Jack and the friends he meets along the way in his adventures.

There is Daisy whose being sets the story in motion. Alvin the wizard who encourages Jack on his journey and teaches him secrets of the realm. Johephra who aids him in his task to save the illusive Cluck from the giant Bartholomu.

There are others who influence the outcome. You will meet them as you travel with Jack and his entourage in their surreal world.

To Kip & Karen,

I think this will help your creek

D. A. Stewart

THE TWISTED TALE OF JACK AND THE BEANSTALK

The Story You've Never Heard

D.A. STEWART

authorHOUSE™

1663 LIBERTY DRIVE, SUITE 200
BLOOMINGTON, INDIANA 47403
(800) 839-8640
WWW.AUTHORHOUSE.COM

First published by AuthorHouse 12/14/05

ISBN: 1-4208-8744-0 (sc)

Printed in the United States of America
Bloomington, Indiana

This book is printed on acid-free paper.

DEDICATION

This book is dedicated to my parents, Ontario and Yolanda Venturi. It is because of them that belief in myself is so deeply instilled. Their love has carried me through the ups and downs in my life, and will be with me till the end of my days.

THE TWISTED TALE OF JACK AND THE BEANSTALK

CHAPTER 1

Once upon a time there was a little boy named Jack. He wasn't a big kid, but his quick mind made up for what he lacked in size. Despite his good nature, he could be a handful for his mother at times.

Ophellia, his mother, was having a really bad day. She was going through menopause, which, as anyone knows, is not fun at the best of times. On this one particular day, the welfare cheque had not arrived as it normally did. She was in dire need. Ophelia had been trying to quit smoking since she could no longer afford it. Since Bingo was out of the question, she had no way to relieve her stress and tension was high in the household. You see, the reserve store had shut down, so cigarettes were too costly now. She looked all through the cupboards and could find no change. Withdrawal was setting in bad. But she did find a jar with a ticket stub in it. On further investigation of this ticket, she realized she had won a cow from the local dairy association draw. She immediately summoned Jack to go into town and retrieve the cow she had won. Just so you know, the cow's name was Daisy. This will be an important factor in the story later on. So please remember her name.

Jack was an obedient little boy for the most part, so he took the ticket stub into town to go and get Daisy. He knew the cow's name, for it was on the ticket. You see, this draw was for a particular cow. Had Jack known the progression of events to follow, he would never had fulfilled his mother's wishes. Daisy would have stayed in the farmer's barn. But Jack, not being a psychic, could not foretell the future. So, on his way he went.

About two hours later in this story, Jack arrived at the edge of town. The little town was called SALEM. It was a picturesque place, with houses all in a row. You see, they had only row housing, due to being a depressed area. Once upon a time, this had been a vital and thriving community.

Ever since the famous salem witch hunts, the witches school of sorcery had shut down. When it closed, most of the students had to move away from home in order to further their careers in this field. So, when that happened, Salem became a sad little oppressed town. I know this sounds like it doesn't belong in the story, but as you will see, it plays an important part.

However, there was a shopkeeper, who had a quaint store around the corner from the local hotel. It was an obscure little shop with two small windows in the front and of course a door. Inside, stood a decrepid old man with a cane, and a parrot named George on his shoulder. He was a bit odd, but very wise in the occult. By the way, this is not Captain Cook reincarnated.

Now, we left Jack at the edge of town, you remember. Well, as luck would have it, when Jack reached the farmer's barn to retrieve his cow-remember her name was Daisy- she was not there. Unfortunately, Daisy had contracted mad cow disease, and had to be destroyed (humanely of course). What was Jack to do now? His mother, Ophellia, would have a fit when he arrived home empty-handed. All the farmer could offer Jack in lieu of the cow was a handful of magic beans, which had been given to him as a gift for favours done, from the Great Sorcerer Alzabar. The little boy gladly accepted these. After all, what else was he to do? Bubba, the farmer, of course with a name like that, was from Tennessee. Bubba, years ago, had done a great favor for the almighty Alzabar. The great sorcerer had rewarded him with a handful of magic beans. Bubba, being from the hills, really didn't have much use for them. A gardener he was not. He couldn't get dandelions to grow even if he used Miracle Grow. So, he put them in a jar, set it on the shelf and forgot about it-till Jack came along! So, being the cunning redneck that he was, he pawned the beans off on Jack, of course. Bubba wasn't a stupid man, so he figured he was just out some old beans that the senile sorcerer had given him, not one of his precious cows. You see, Bubba had lied to Jack. Daisy was out in the far field grazing. She was a special cow, but no one knew it except one person in the town.

Now, back to Jack again. I know, we keep losing him, but we always manage to find him. As Jack strolled through Salem, he came across the old man's shop-remember the occult guy- well, that's who we're talking about now. His name was Alvin. I know that's not a typical sorcerer's name, but Alvin was anything but typical. Jack was a little apprehensive about entering the tiny shop, for his mother, remember her, Ophillia, had warned him never to go there. But, curiosity had gotten the best of Jack and of course, guess where he headed! Smack dab in the middle of trouble!!

Alvin was quite approachable, as Jack found out and they struck up a conversation. As the story of the beans came to light, Alvin's eyes lit up. He wanted them very badly, for he and only he, knew what they were. Jack, not being quite the fool that he looked, realized this, and figured out that he had some bargaining leverage. So, as time went on, they bartered back and forth till the two of them came to an agreement. Jack would give Alvin the magician the beans, and would receive $100.00 for them. Well, Jack thought he had won the super 7 lottery when this happened. His mother would be so proud of him for what he had accomplished. She would be able to buy her cigarettes and go to bingo and get off his back. Jack thought all was well in his world. Little did he know what would happen next!!!

Jack arrived home with money in hand and Ophillia was absolutely thrilled. She gave her beloved son $10.00 and told him to go out and have a goodtime- you earned it! Well, guess what? Jack did go out, but so did Ophillia. She got herself all gussied up and went to the local hotel to party. She definitely found a party- but we won't go there. This is a clean story and we'll keep it that way! All I can tell you is that she found someone and guess what? She never came home for-we're not sure yet for how long. We'll see what happens as time goes by.

When Jack arrived home, he found the house empty. He knew what had happened-he'd been there before with Ophillia. Eventually, she always comes back. He was used to this, so he didn't worry too much. As long as she didn't come home pregnant, everything was o.k. Jack wasn't too fond of being alone, so he did what he had done before, but with a bit of a change. Instead of going to stay with his uncle Willard, as he usually did when Ophillia pulled one of her stunts, he thought he would approach the mysterious, but friendly wizard he had met, Alvin. He imagined it would be really cool to live with a magician for a while. Anyway, it seemed like a good idea at the time. So away Jack went-back into Salem. He didn't mind the three mile walk. After all, it was a beautiful day. If you thought this is confusing so far, wait till you read the rest of this! This is where the story gets a little strange.

Surprisingly to Jack, Alvin welcomed him with open arms. He wasn't weird or anything; he was just a lonely old wizard. As time went on, Jack and Alvin became good friends. The old wizard decided it was time for Jack to know about the magic beans. Little did Jack know, this was to be his destiny. Alvin instructed Jack to go into the backyard and plant the beans beside the twisted tree growing out back. Jack did so, for he wanted to please the wizard. He seemed to know there was something special about the old man, but he wasn't quite sure what it was. Don't worry, he definitely will find out! The story doesn't end here.

Well, it only took a couple of days and out of the earth, where the beans had been planted emerged a massive beanstalk. It reached heights that no one could imagine. The giant green stem reached the clouds above and beyond. Jack was amazed. He had never seen anything quite like it. Emerging from the stalk of this great plant life were branches, creating a ladder effect all the way up. The beanstalk reminded him of the triffids-in the book "Day Of The Triffids"-just in case you haven't read it. Well, Jack thought, this was definitely intriguing. Further investigation was positively in the foreseeable future. The wizard, noticing the look on Jack's face, knew what would happen next. After all, you have to realize, he was a wizard ! He took Jack in the quaint shop and proceeded to tell him about the magic beanstalk. So, here goes! I don't think you've ever heard this side of the story before. If you have, you're more twisted than I am!

Way up in the high atmosphere, above the clouds, lives a giant alien. In his castle exists a mammoth chicken. The great chicken, whose name is Cluck, is very precious to the giant. By the way, in case I haven't told you, the giant's name is Bartholomu-just in case you wanted to know. Every day, at precisely four o'clock, Cluck goes to the kitchen and makes Bartholomu's favorite chicken soup-What else! This is no ordinary chicken soup. It has magical ingredients only Cluck knows about. Without this special broth, Bartholomu could not sustain his size. Should he lose his size, his powers as a giant alien would disappear. That would not be acceptable at all! Of course, there is more to this chicken than meets the eye. But we'll talk about that later. You have to realize Bartholomu's home had to be massive in order to accommodate his size and his high standard of living. He liked the good life and could afford it, so long as Cluck was in the picture. We'll get to that part eventually. After all, he did live in the affluent part of town and taxes were high. His alien "Rock till you drop" parties lasted for days sometimes. That wasn't cheap either. Here's where Cluck comes into the picture big time. You see, Cluck was a very special chicken. In her room was an extremely large nesting box. This is where Cluck would lay purple boxes. These purple boxes were filled with thousand dollar bills. Every morning, Bartholomu would go the massive

nest box and collect the boxes. Then, he would proceed
to the local bank and make his daily deposits. I'll tell
you-this boy was not broke. He could make Donald
Trump look like a pauper! So you see, Cluck was very
important to Bartholomu for many reasons. There was
no way that chicken was going anywhere!

Now I know you're still wondering where Daisy-
remember the cow- comes into this picture. Don't
worry, we'll get to her eventually. But for now, back to
our story.

That night, as Jack lay sleeping, he dreamed of riches
beyond his belief. If he could only get his hands on
that ridiculous chicken. Of course, he realized , he had
to capture Cluck alive. For whoever had possession of
Cluck would be able to collect the boxes. So, he must
devise a plan to capture Cluck. Now, remember, one
must always have a plan B-just in case plan A doesn't
go quite right.

The very next day, Jack packed his camping gear-he
didn't know how long this would take- so he should at
least be prepared to stay a few days. He double-checked
to make sure he had all his supplies-tent, lantern, food,
water (the town could be called Walkerton you never
know) visa (never travel without it) and his air miles
card-just in case. You never know when you might
need it. He had enough air miles built up, just in case
he had to take the red-eye home. He climbed the giant
beanstalk step by step. Really! How high could this
thing be? He was about to find out. Halfway up, he

found a giant leaf. It was getting dark, so Jack decided
to set up camp for the night. After a good night's sleep,
for the leaf was a Serta Posturepedic pillowtop, he set
out for Bartholomu's castle.

Upon his arrival at the top of the beanstalk, Jack
discovered a whole new world. The wizard had not told
him about this part. Fields were green and lush, birds
sang, and the sun was bright and shining. This was a
happy place. No row housing here!

As he went along his way, Jack met up with a giant
rooster named Johephra. Johephra was a sad rooster
though. Loneliness had taken it's toll on poor Johephra
over his few short years. He had been looking for a
suitable mate for a long, long time. He wasn't get any
younger and he didn't want to wait too long to start a
family. And, let's face it; there weren't too many giant
chickens to choose from. Actually, there weren't any
except for guess who? Cluck, of course. The great ice
age had made them almost extinct. He longed to see
her. He had only heard about her through the grapevine, but had never been able to catch a glimpse of her.
Apparently, she was pretty hot stuff. A real fox!!! Of
course, Bartholomu knew this of her, so he kept her well
hidden from the rest of the world. Should he ever lose
Cluck, his fortune would be gone. You see, Bartholomu
had made some bad investments and he did have a bit
of a gambling problem. The local casino loved him, but
it didn't do him any good at all. Losing Cluck would
be his demise.

Anyway, back to Jack again. After Johephra had confided in Jack, the two of them came to a mutual decision. They would become partners. It seemed logical at the time, don't you agree. After all, Johephra had a little more insite into chickens than Jack did. If he didn't, there's something definitely wrong with that boy! Putting their contract in writing would make it binding in a court of law-so that's what they did. So, as you can guess, Jack and Johephra went to see a lawyer and had him draw up a legal and binding contract. This contract contained the following terms:

1. Jack would have legal guardianship of Cluck
2. Johephra would reside with Cluck (of course, he would have to marry her.). We have to keep this story morally correct. After all, we do not want an R rating.
3. Jack would get one half of the money in the purple boxes and Johephra and Cluck would get the other half.
4. They would both reside on the same property, each having their own home
5. A top investment broker would be hired to ensure their financial future is kept secure.
6. Should anything happen to either of them, the other would inherit the deceased's estate.
7. Jack would provide for Ophillia for the rest of her life.

8. A proper legal will would be drawn up so as to avoid probate tax. Besides, even in this story the government will get you if it can.

This agreement seemed fair to both Jack and Johephra. So, the two of them went on their way to rescue Cluck, Johephra's beloved. She didn't know it yet, but she will! After all, Johephra was a real catch as far as giant roosters go. He knew how to keep his chicks smiling!!! We won't delve into that any farther. Your imagination can do the rest. By the way, get your mind out of the gutter. Johephra was, if nothing else, a gentleman with a lot of class. He'd been around the block a few times, so he knew what to do!! So away the daring duo went.

On reaching the castle gates, they noticed a sign. It said: "FORECLOSURE SALE". Adding to their surprise, the castle gates were wide open. Well, didn't this make life a whole lot easier? You see, no one knew about Cluck's problem. She had come down with a bad case of "purple box syndrome". Bartholomu had taken Cluck to the finest giant chicken doctors in the land, but to no avail. As everyone knows, except Jack of course-sometimes he could be a bit of a dough head-in the world of giant chickens, every three years the chicken must mate with a giant rooster. This was common knowledge in the feathered community. But, giant roosters are pretty scarce these days. Have you seen any lately? See what I mean. Jack and Johephra sat down, brainstormed, and came up with a plan. They would go to the bank and buy the castle. Bartholomu was no longer a problem. Since the purple boxes weren't there any more, he had lost his size and alien powers. Turning into a troll, he had sadly left his residence and had gone off to find a nice bridge to live under. Ask any troll that was ever a giant alien-you need a bridge. Now that's having a bad day! Don't you agree?

On the way to the bank, the pair stopped at a local" bed and breakfast" and booked two rooms for the night. Both wanted to get cleaned up and look presentable to meet the banker. Two rooms were necessary. You know how gossip is in a small community. After all, they were two different species and what would everyone think. Jack had brought his visa gold card with him. The saying "never travel without it" had never been truer. Both had a good night's sleep and woke refreshed and raring to go the next morning.

The bank manager was anxious to unload Bartholomu's castle, as long as Jack could cover the debt owing on it. Jack had a very good credit rating and of course, his visa gold card. So, the deal was closed and all parties got what they wanted. Now, all they had to do was find Cluck. The castle was useless to them, so they donated it to the poor for a homeless shelter. I thought that was pretty decent of them-don't you?

On entering Bartholomu's ex-home, they were amazed at the extravagance of it all. Marble floors, gold banisters, magnificent crystal chandeliers hanging from elaborately decorated ceilings. It was a feast for the eyes. Even Debbie Travis could outdo this place. It was like living on Rodeo Drive , but more exquisite. Unfortunately for them, this was not the world they wanted.

Jack and Johephra called and called throughout the house, but no luck. It seemed as though Cluck was gone. But something stirred inside Johephra and he knew she was there somewhere. He could sense it. Chickens and roosters can do this you know. If you didn't, I can understand it. You're not a chicken or a rooster are you? If you are, we should do lunch. I have an agent that would be happy to meet with you.

In a room barely big enough for her, Johephra found his beloved Cluck. When their eyes met, it was love at first sight. Cluck smiled sweetly and Johephra was caught-hook, line, and sinker. They knew they were meant for each other. He had heard she was a looker, but Sophia Loren move over, here comes Cluck!

Arm in arm, they ventured forth. Such a smile hadn't been seen on Johephra's face in a long time. He was one happy camper! The three of them strolled through the fields of green, savoring the fragrant scent of the beautiful flowers along the way. Johephra noticed a special rose not far away. He picked this perfect white rose and gave it to Cluck as a symbol of his undying love for her. She smiled sweetly, demurely batting her eyelashes for him in return. Chickens do that you know. Of course, Cluck's lashes weren't overly large. They were just right thought Johephra. After all, he didn't want a Tammy

Faye Baker on his hands! That would be a little over the top. Anyway, we're getting a little distracted here. This is not a love story-just a drama in disguise.

Dusk was setting in by now, so they set up camp for the night. Jack in his tent, Johephra in his, and Cluck in hers. Johephra and Cluck were not married yet, so being together was definitely out of the question. She wanted to wear white on her wedding day, not purple, red, or any other color. So that was that.

The next morning they set out bright and early for the long journey home down the beanstalk. After reaching the bottom, Jack took out a chainsaw from his pack and proceeded to cut down the giant stalk. You see, that was part of the deal with the banker. He did not want new people moving into his community. If that happened, one would end up with factories, smog, pollution, an increase in the crime rate, and worst of all, more government control. This would disrupt their whole way of life. Out of the question.

Jack made sure they all went to thank Alvin-remember him-the wizard. After all, if it weren't for him, none of this would have been possible. The great wizard was happy to see them and was elated to hear of their successful journey. Alvin would never hurt for anything again. This Jack promised him. Let's face it, Jack owed Alvin big time!

When Jack arrived home, he found Ophillia had returned-none the worse for wear. I guess the party had agreed with her. She hugged Jack tightly for she had missed him after all. Ophillia was a very warm and giving person for the most part. She cooked them all a tasty supper, with an extremely luscious dessert-double strawberry cream cheesecake-Jack's favourite. After supper, they all retired to the living room and Ophillia listened to the tale of their amazing journey. She was ecstatic to hear they would not have to depend on welfare any longer.

The next day, the whole crew put their plan in motion. Real estate agents were more than happy to show them many beautiful properties. Not being quite sure where they wanted to live, a decision was made to rent for now. Down the road was a picturesque one hundred acre farm with many different fruit trees, fertile fields of hay, oats and corn. The barn was perfect. It had a quaint, but spacious stable area, white Gallagher vinyl fencing, and two beautiful homes on the property. It was the perfect place for Jack, Ophillia, Cluck and Johephra. This was worth giving a try! Since they hadn't much furniture, calling U-Haul was not necessary. So they packed their belongings into the old pick-up out back and away they went to their new life. This had to be better than the old one. It sucked really bad!

After settling into their new homes, Jack had one more errand to run. Away he went to Bubba's house. Remember Bubba-the redneck farmer from Tennessee. Yeah! That's him. Now this is the part of the story where Daisy comes into the picture. See, I told you she'd be back. I'll bet you didn't believe me. Fooled you, didn't I? Jack purchased Daisy from farmer Bubba. Let's face reality here, Bubba liked money more than he did Daisy. Jack had made him an offer he couldn't refuse. Daisy was quite happy to go with Jack. She knew that Bubba wasn't that attached to her anyway. At least Jack was a good dude.

A month went by and life was good on the farm. Cluck and Johephra had a big lavish wedding. Cluck wanted this and this story had better accommodate her. After all, where do you think those purple boxes came from. All their feathered friends came-the Emu family, the starling clan, the crow tribe, the Kingfisher family, and so on. It was the social event of the season. Even Ivana Trump couldn't have topped this one.

After the festivities had died down, Jack, being an ambitious fellow, decided to take Daisy to the "Royal Winter Fair" in Toronto, Canada. Daisy had the looks, the poise, the sophistication, and the body (ooh! la! la!) to turn heads. She had it all. So, as you can guess, airline reservations were made through Bernard, the local travel agent for Travel Masters. Tickets were booked and Jack and Daisy were to leave on the fifteenth of November.

Daisy wanted to make sure she was in peak condition for the big show, so she took out a membership at the local Y.M.C.A. and started working out. Let me tell you, she was one hot mama when November came. Ain't nothing gonna touch this chick!

As expected, Daisy stole the show and came home with trophies and ribbons galore-say nothing of the prestige that goes along with it. Her reputation preceded her on arriving home. You see, this had been broadcast on national television coast to coast. Farmers were lined up for miles along the white rail fence with their best bulls. Strutting her stuff as she inspected the fine specimens before her, Daisy's eye caught sight of Toronado, the great Spanish bull from Toledo. (Ohio, of course). Remember, we are in the U.S. After picking her mate, Daisy strolled back to the barn. After all, it was not ladylike to appear too anxious. A few days later, Jack went to the local auction house and purchased some of the best heifers in the land.

Now let's jump ahead a couple of years or we'll be here forever. The herd had grown in size and the farm was getting a little crowded and such with all the animals. The two families decided a bigger place was in order. Even Cluck and Johephra were feeling a bit claustrophobic and needed more space. Cluck had had twins two years ago. I'll tell you, that's enough for anyone in my books- I don't know about you! Money was no object, so it's go big or stay at home! Texas seemed like a good state to check out. Flipping through the pages of the national real estate book, Jack and Johephra found the perfect place. This they would buy not rent. Believing in a democratic society as he did, Jack held a family meeting with everyone, including Daisy and Toronado. All were in agreement for the move.

The very next day, Jack made the all-important call and a deal was made. It took a while to get ready for the move, but in time all was done. The old pick-up was gone-the scrap yard had it now- so they called National Transport and the necessary arrangements were made for the move. Bernard, their travel agent, got in touch with American Airlines and booked them all in first class of course. Let's face it, with that kind of money, why would you fly economy? Well, two weeks went by and it was finally time to go. A big going away party had been held for them and all the people in the land had come. Jack and his family would be sadly missed, but you have to do what you have to do.

Arriving at Dallas International was quite the scene. Daisy turned heads everywhere she went. Ophillia really got off on all those good-looking cowboys, all sexy in their cowboy boots and all. She had turned into quite the knockout herself after getting on the television program "The Swan". You'd be amazed at what cosmetic plastic surgery can do these days. She looked twenty years younger. I wish she would adopt me-I could use the help, believe me! The limousine picked them all up and drove them to their new home. The place was a sight to see! A real Texas spread – ten thousand acres of prime land with two magnificent homes, one for each of them. You remember the contract that Jack and Johephra signed- it had to be honored.

Jack eventually joined the oil barons association, went to all the high society parties, and let's be realistic, had the good life. Jack and Ophillia, Cluck and Johephra, Daisy and Toronado now reside at Southfork and live happily to this day in Dallas, Texas.

CHAPTER 2

When we last left Jack, Ophillia, Cluck, Johephra, Daisy and Toronado, they were living the good life at Southfork in Dallas, Texas. Well, they're still there and still living quite well I might add.

As it turned out, the investment broker Jack and Johephra hired did extremely well for them. Their mutual funds flourished, real estate markets soared, and beef and oil prices were at an all time high. All was well almost. Due to their enormous wealth, for the purple boxes were still coming, tax write-offs were definitely a must. It was quite a dilemma for them.

Since everyone was involved a family meeting was in order. The investment broker-we'll call him Billy-Bob arrived on schedule to present his ideas. You know he was a Texan- with a name like that-of course. Daisy and Toronado arrived. Daisy looked as glamorous as ever. Texas definitely agreed with her. Toronado, still the good-looking debonair bull that he was, accompanied her. On hearing the doorbell – it was actually a chime that played the chicken song- Ulio, the sexually challenged Latin butler, proceeded to welcome the remainder of the guests. Cluck looked ravishing in her purple ensemble. Purple, being her colour brought out the yellow in her eyes. Johephra, looking as dashing as ever, was also present. They had left the chicks at home with the nanny. This was not a party. Serious decisions had to be made this night. Cluck and Johephra must be able to focus on the task at hand, not be chasing chicks all over the house. Quick and Quack, the twins, were a little on the rambunctious side. Besides, the nanny they had hired, Big Bird, was great with the children. He understood and managed them very well. He should, he was a giant chicken himself. I know you have seen him on Sesame Street, but since the cancellation of the program by CBS, he had to find alternate work. This is how Big Bird had come to be a nanny-and a very good one at that. Remember, in chapter 1, giant chickens had become extinct due to the great ice age, except for Cluck. Well, Big Bird had literally fallen through the cracks and managed to survive. Giant chickens have an extremely long life span you know. No need for Joan Rivers's antics here!

Once all had arrived, cocktails were served; conversation was plenty, everyone discussing the latest events of the day. Dinner was served in the formal dining room.

It was quite a feast with salmon almandine as the main course. Let's face it, would you serve beef or fowl with a cow and a chicken as guests? Especially giant ones at that! Those beaks could do a lot of damage should they be provoked. Dessert was, of course, Jack's favourite; remember from chapter 1, strawberry cream double cheesecake. After their scrumptious meal all retired to the drawing room for the all important meeting. That's why they were all here, wasn't it? You know it, I know it, and now they know it!

We will get away from the present for the moment. We must delve into the past in order to bring this story into context. No, I don't have dementia; I just need to do this.

At that time in this century, Faramount Pictures had a bit of a financial problem. Well, it wasn't quite as small as they would like it to be. You see, they were in bankruptcy mode and unless they had a backer, they would have to fold. The last picture they had produced "The Day The Chicken Stood Still" turned out to be a flop. Millions had been invested, as it is very costly to film overseas- in Romania to be exact. The euro had soared in value and the American dollar was down fifty percent due to inflation. Now, do you see where I am going with this? Of course not. You didn't write this story. How would you know? Let's face it; the whole thing makes no sense anyhow.

Now, back to the present in our story. Billy-Bob suggested that the family buy out Faramount Pictures.

They could get a really good deal on a takeover bid as long as the price was right. Open door number three. All agreed this was a fabulous idea.. The necessary documents were drawn up and a generous offer was made to Faramount. The movie studio, in case you didn't know what Faramount was, jumped at the offer. They were absolutely ecstatic about it! Of course, there were conditions attached. You've heard of attachments before, but not like this one. Toronado would be appointed head of the board of directors for the studio, with Billy-Bob as the financial advisor. After all, hadn't Billy-Bob done a great job for the family in the past? Well, why blow a good thing when you don't have to.

Daisy had always wanted to get into acting and, you guessed it, this was her chance. The studio had agreed that if Daisy had it in her, she would definitely have a part in their next film. Which film? We don't know that yet. But we will soon. Daisy was no fool. She knew she would have to work very hard for this and would have to take acting lessons. This seemed fair enough considering the opportunity before her. So, as planned, in this story anyway, she worked extremely hard everyday for two months straight. Her audition was coming up shortly and she wanted to be fully prepared for it. She learned the script inside and out. No one was going to mess this up for her, not even herself. Well, her big day came and she blew their socks off!!! They had never seen such a natural, especially for a cow. From this point on in the story we will be using the term bovine. After all, one must use the proper etiquette when one is living in the upper echelon of society. There! That fixes that.

For a movie to be great, it must have exceptional writers. So the best were hired to come up with an academy award winning movie script. It took about four months and finally they had a winner. The movie would be called "The Day Of The Bovine". It seemed appropriate at the time and Daisy was perfect for the part. The script suited her to a tee. She absolutely loved it and buried herself in her work. Toronado and Daisy had no little ones as of yet, so she had the time and her family wouldn't suffer from her busy schedule. All in all, it worked out very well. The movie was produced by the Feelgood Corporation and it took off. Daisy ended up being nominated for an academy award for best actress. She was absolutely ecstatic over the whole thing. The bovine community applauded her for her work. Daisy was their idol. Well, Daisy did win the award for best actress, along with Ophra Windy as best supporting actress. All in all, it was a great time in their lives.

Toronado was no slouch himself. As it turned out he was a brilliant business bull. He had gone into the export business with Spain and things took off from there. Of course, the country he dealt with had to be Spain for two predominantly good reasons. One, it was his homeland, so he knew how to work with the people there and two, he was a Spanish bull from Spain, so it had to fit with the story. On one of his many trips abroad, he met the ambassador of the country, El Figaro, who was greatly impressed with Toronado. As it turned out, El Figaro had been looking for someone to replace the foreign affairs minister in his cabinet. He thought Toronado would fit the bill perfectly. Now, Toronado, being of Spanish descent, but having American citizenship, could not be their foreign affairs minister, so a position was made available for him as international liaison with Spain and the United States. Toronado was quite pleased about this and El Figaro was one hundred percent satisfied that he had made the right choice. All in all, I think it was pretty darn good in this lifetime. How many bulls have you seen in politics lately? Remember, I said bulls, not bull.

I know you might think we forgot about Johephra and the others, but not to worry. We'll get to the rest of them soon. Now it is Johephra's turn. He had entered the world of politics also, but not in the same fashion as Toronado. Johephra had become the president of the association for feathered friends called "World Wide Fowl ". He had taken chickens to new heights. No longer did they stay in a pen out in the barnyard and lay eggs and such- whatever chickens do, and roosters of course. The feathered community now had voting rights, their own party in the government and had a say in their future. For all his great work in the chicken industry, Johephra was nominated for the Nobel Peace Prize. He won this hands down. You know, he deserved this. Do you know any other chickens that have accomplished as much in their lifetime?

Ophillia, you remember her, Jack's mother, well she's still around. She finally met Mr. Right. His name was Lefty Wigmor. He was a tall, good looking, charming, and rich, of course. Let's face it, the elite have to stay together. Things went well for the couple. They married a few months later. The wedding was held at Southfork and it was quite the social event. Even El Figaro and his entourage were there. Everyone who was anyone attended. After the ceremony was over and everyone had left the reception, it was time for the couple to depart for their honeymoon. Ophillia had never been to Cleveland, Ohio. So guess where they went? That wasn't hard to figure out, was it? Now, I don't know about you, but if I got married and my husband took me to Cleveland for my honeymoon, I can guarantee there would be a lawyer involved in there eventually. But to each his own. I have never figured out what is in Cleveland to make anyone go there, but maybe there is something about the place that we don't know.

After a few years of marriage, things weren't quite so smooth between Ophillia and Lefty. He wanted children and that was out of the question for her. Remember, she went on the television show "The Swan". This is why she looked so young. Ophillia never did tell Lefty her true age. And you'll never know it either. We are not telling you in this story. It's not important anyway. So, why bother? Since children were a no-no, and oh yes, Ophillia still had a bit of her wild ways in her, Lefty was not a happy camper. I know I've used this saying before in the story, but I couldn't think of anything else. Besides, it fits. To make a long story short, Ophillia and Lefty end up in divorce court in front of Judge Jody. All assets were divided according to Texas law; Ophillia went back to Southfork and Lefty, well he just left. A year later in this book, the families' get a visitor from home. It is Bernard, the real estate agent from chapter 1. Ophillia and Bernard hit it off pretty well. They seemed like a perfect match. I know Ophillia blew it once, but as the saying goes, if you don't succeed, try and try again. And that she did.

Don't worry, we haven't lost Jack. We just put him in safe storage till we needed him again. After all, he is the main character in the book. Jack finally met his true love, Mildred. She was a petite divorcee with flaming red hair and the greenest eyes he had ever seen. It's a good thing Jack loved children because Mildred had a slew of them. Twelve to be precise, from a previous marriage. She lived comfortably, but not excessively in her very large shoe with all her children. I'd tell you the name of these children, but with twelve of them, I'd be here all day. Besides, who can remember all twelve? We'll just call them one through twelve for now. That will make life a little easier. I think this story is confusing enough already, don't you? They courted for two years. Jack had to be sure of things before he took the big step into marriage. He got along great with the children one through twelve inclusive. After their courtship, Jack and Mildred finally married. It was quite the occasion. Everyone was happy for Jack, for he had been searching for someone for a long time. For him, Mildred was worth the wait. The entire family now lived at Southfork. Mildred was in awe of the estate. She had never in her life thought she would end up so happy and in such a place. It was a little confusing at first, with all these kids and the twins, but all got along famously. The twins, Quick and Quack, would play with the children most of the day, which gave Jack and Mildred some time to themselves. Of course, a cook had to be hired. Feeding all these children was an all day job in itself. They advertised through the local media and found the perfect chef. Her name was Julia Shilds. She came highly recommended, with an excellent resume. Jack and Mildred couldn't have been happier. With Big Bird watching over the crew and Julia looking after the meals, life was a whole lot easier for Jack and Mildred.

Time passed and it wasn't long before Quick and Quack must go to school. After all, even chickens need an education. So, it was decided that the twins should attend Mother Goose's School for Giant Chickens. All the famous giant chickens had gone there. It was an excellent choice thought Cluck and Johephra. And they were so right. How many schools do you know that cater to this species? She's the only one that I know of. If you've heard of any others, please let me know, and

I will pass the information on to them. It would be greatly appreciated just in case things don't work out with Mother Goose.

One fine day, on their way home from school, Quick and Quack noticed a sign on the roadside. It said "Magic Forest". The twins had been told of this place, but had never seen it. Cluck and Johephra had warned them never to go there. A lot of strange things happened in this forest. They didn't call it a magic forest for nothing. Well, kids being kids, and chickens being notoriously curious, more than other species, you can guess where they headed. Right on! In the Magic Forest. Neither of them was sure of what they would find, but if you know most kids, this place was definitely worth checking out. So, away they went. Once inside the enchanted forest- we'll use this term, because the word magic is getting kind of old- the two were amazed at what they saw.

Over on the far side of a lush green meadow were unicorns grazing peacefully. Quick and Quack had never seen anything so beautiful in all their lives. Silvery white horses with golden manes, tails, and a horn to die for. They looked so peaceful in this place. One of the unicorns, Gabriel, noticed the new visitors. He trotted over and asked them what they were doing here. No one had entered the enchanted forest in a long time. So new chickens, especially giant ones, were somewhat of a curiosity. Anyway, Gabriel brought them over and introduced them to the others. These unicorns were so friendly and very helpful to the chicks. Gabriel's unicorn friend-we have to write it this way because Gabriel had other friends that were not unicorns- Boris, started telling Quick and Quack about all the sights to see here. The chicks were told to never mind the grumpy old groundhog, Oliver, should they come across him.. He was all talk most of the time. Anyway he liked giant chickens, so the two had no worries. They were instructed to follow the yellow brick road ahead. This would lead them to Zucchini Valley. It wasn't that far, only about a fifteen-minute walk – at unicorn speed. But, no matter, the twins would go.

This strange valley sounded pretty interesting to them. Along their way, just after the long bend in the fork of the road- they were to stay to the right, by the way- the twins encountered an odd looking creature. It had the shape of a pig with a snout that resembled an orchid-hence a snork. The snork seemed friendly enough, for he smiled and greeted Quick and Quack in such a nice way. He asked them where they were going. The twins proceeded to tell the snork, whose name happens to be Truffles, that they were told by the unicorn to follow the yellow brick road. They were headed to Zucchini Valley. Truffles knew the place. He had been there once for a garden party that had been put on by the mayor of Pickletown, a small community close by. It had been quite an occasion. He told them should they get a chance to visit Pickletown, they should do so. It was a picturesque place with all the cucumbers in a row. After having an informative conversation with the snork, the twins went on their way. It wasn't long before they arrived at Zucchini Valley. The two couldn't believe their eyes. It was a beautiful here, but a little strange. Very different from anything they had ever seen, that's for sure. All the houses were round. Even the streets had no corners. Everything went in circles. Such an odd little place. You've heard of the circle of life. Where do you think that saying came from? Zucchini Valley of course. No one ever knew this before, but then how many of you have ever been to the magic forest?

The two travelers meandered through the streets of the tiny town till they came to a small internet café named Netscope. Inside the café, according to the rules of the valley, everything was round –the chairs, tables, even the walls. They had been traveling a while, so they thought they would quench their thirst before moving on. The proprietors, Bert and Ernie (remember them from Sesame Street) welcomed the strangers with open arms. Quick and Quack felt very comfortable here. They thought this was a really cool place and wished there was a place like this where they came from. The chocolate sundae floats they ordered were delicious. Nothing at home ever tasted so good! On leaving the premises, Bert asked them if they had seen the giant walnut yet. It was law in this valley that all visitors must report in on arrival. They were to go to the immigration office and ask for Walley, the giant talking walnut. He would record their statistics and issue them their passport. Without this document, the twins could not continue their journey down the yellow brick road. Bert gave them directions on how to get there. They were to turn right on Turnip lane, go two Squash blocks, then left on Rutabaga drive. When they see the sign for Sphere's, turn left again on Lettuce Leaf Street. Here, they would find the immigration office. It was a large round; of course, tan coloured building in the shape of -you guessed it- a walnut. The pair should ask for Walley. Quick and Quack followed the directions given to the letter and lo and behold there it was! The biggest walnut they had ever seen in their lives. Walley met them at the door, for Ernie had called him on his cell phone (issued by Zucchini Telecom, which, like us, charge too high a rate) and told him they were coming. This Walley fellow was very accommodating. He was a large walnut, as nuts go, but very soft-spoken and jovial. It was a pleasure to meet him the twins thought and quite an honour, for Walley was the Grand Pubba of the Giant Nut and Pecan Association. After receiving the proper documents, Quick and Quack were on their way.

The sign just outside Zucchini Valley said: "Pickletown 1 mile ". This didn't seem that far away, not for giant chickens anyhow, so the dynamic duo headed west. The yellow brick road would take them directly there. This place was quite different from Zucchini Valley. Everything here was oblong. What other shape did you think it would be with a name like Pickletown?

The streets were long and narrow, for this were an English town. As told to them by Truffles the snork, all the cucumbers were in a row. White cabbage lights lined the streets, orange carrots stood on each corner, mailboxes were fluorescent pink and yellow, and every different colour of the rainbow was here. It was something to see! After taking in all the sights, the two ventured into a quaint little shop where they thought they would do lunch. The smell of warm crescent rolls fresh out of an easy-bake oven filled the air. Quick and Quack hadn't realized how hungry they really were. A good lunch would definitely do the trick. During this time, the townspeople had started to gather around them. Quick and Quack hadn't noticed them immediately. Let's be real here! When you're that hungry, nothing else matters. The stomach rules!

When their appetites were satisfied, they looked up and saw the townspeople around them. Strange little creatures they thought. Green, blue, orange, purple, red, pink, all the colours were here. And all different shapes and sizes. Some were taller than others, some were minute little things. One odd character stood out from the rest. He was gray in colour, slightly rounded, and had one large stump where two feet protruded. You see, he could never be completely circular, this was after all Pickletown. As it turned out, his name was Magic Mushroom. He was the mayor of Pickletown. Now, are you catching on to the colour theme? If you're not, I'm not telling you! I don't think your mother would appreciate it. You'll have to figure this one out on your own. Magic Mushroom told them of a place where all the real magic happens. This truly sparked their curiosity and you know exactly where the two headed for. Wouldn't you? Of course, we have to follow the yellow brick road to get there. That's pretty obvious, don't you think. If you haven't surmised this so far, you've got more problems than I thought. And that's as far as we'll go with that. Like anything else, risks are involved. And so, life is no different in the enchanted forest.

Magic Mushroom had told them to beware of the evil sorcerer Jerry Springtime. He was a mean little fellow with two heads, long tentacles for arms, and a very nasty disposition. Kind of like a medium sized squid on a bad day. If he ever asked the mirror "Mirror, mirror on the wall, who's the fairest of them all?" I sure as heck wouldn't want to know the answer to that one! Talk about putting someone in a bad mood real quick! Anyway, back to our travellers. Quick and Quack told Magic Mushroom they would keep a keen look out for the sorcerer and avoid him at all costs. I know, I wouldn't want to see something that ugly first thing in the morning or anytime actually. And off they went down the yellow brick road.

When you were a kid, wouldn't you have loved an adventure like this? But then, you couldn't have because I wasn't around at that time. Well, enough said, back to our saga.

An hour later in our story, Quick and Quack did not realize they had taken a wrong turn in the road. Had they noticed the sign a little ways back "Wrong Turn" the two would not have ventured where they did. This place was a scary one. Crooked trees with twisted limbs lined the side of the road, and the sounds of frogs were everywhere. On top of that the frogs couldn't even stay on key. This was really hard on the ears. As it turns out, the pair had landed smack dab in the middle of "Bad Echo Village ". They were no houses here, just a whole lot of frogs that couldn't sing. And don't tell me you haven't been there before. I know different! Magic Mushroom had warned them about this. They had better get out of here before the evil sorcerer would hear of their whereabouts. This was a little too close for comfort. The twins turned back and hurried out of there- and real quick I might add!

Quick and Quack got out of there just in the nick of time. As they passed the sign "Bad Echo Village Exit ", Jerry Springtime, the evil sorcerer, came out after them. True to Magic Mushroom's words, he was definitely some ugly! The twins had lucked out, for Jerry Springtime's powers were non-existent outside of Bad Echo Village. They would pay more attention to directions the next time. After all, they still had to get back home sometime in this story!

The two proceeded down the yellow brick road not knowing just where they were headed this time. Magic Mushroom did not know what lay past his immediate area. He wasn't exactly what you would call a world traveler. Let's face it, with a name like Magic Mushroom, what else do you expect!

A few chicken miles down the yellow brick road, Quick and Quack came to a city limit sign. The sign said, "Welcome to Gumdrop City ". This sounded pretty interesting to them. This definitely had to be investigated. After all, remember how curious chickens are. As the twins entered the city, they noticed how colourful this place was. Even more so than Pickletown. Here, everything was made of gumdrops – the houses, the stores, the streets. This was an amazing place! The people jovially bounced up and down the avenues, smiling and as pleasant as could be. They sure were a chubby little bunch. After all, if you lived in a place where gumdrops ruled, you just know Slimfast doesn't live here. You see, this town came about when the local volcano erupted and spewed out thousands of gumdrops. It just so happened; all the gumdrops fell to the ground in the perfect locations. What no one knew was that these gumdrops were architectural gumdrops. They automatically would fall into place. For houses, schools, shops, churches, offices. Pretty cool place, don't you think! All the streets were named for flavors. So, if you were an orange gumdrop, you lived on Citrus Avenue. If you were a red gumdrop, you lived on Strawberry lane. And so on and so on… These two were having quite the adventure, don't you think. Wouldn't you have liked to have been to these places when you were a kid? I know, some of us have visited Magic Mushroom and been to some colourful places during that visit, but to try it as a straight person would be really cool! I know, some of you might think I have visited Magic Mushroom after reading this story, but in actuality, I have never been there- and don't plan to in the future. Just so we get the facts straight!!

After a very nice visit, Quick and Quack merrily went on their way. You know which way they went, of course. If not, you have not been following the story very well. THE YELLOW BRICK ROAD! The path twisted and turned for a few more giant chicken miles. We do miles in this story. We haven't gone metric yet here. Let's keep this simple.

After rounding the next bend, the twins came upon three little brick houses. They were surprised to see bricks in this saga. Quick knocked on door number one, and lo and behold, the cutest little pig answered. Remember the story of the three little pigs and the big bad wolf- well, guess who lived here! Pinky, Porky, and Miss Piggy. Each had a house of their own. After all, the story must remain morally correct. Miss Piggy had not married Kermit as of yet. He had left her to pursue his career in show business and would come back for her when he had made his fortune. So, she waited for him, for Kermit had always been true to his word when it came to Miss Piggy. Pinky and Porky were her cousins three times removed. Family must stick together. And so they did. Quick and Quack had a hot cup of tea with the three little pigs and discussed the events of the fairy tale that they had originally been in. Quack asked his hosts whatever happened to the big bad wolf. The trio proceeded to tell them his story. By the way, his name was Harry. You know why that name, I presume. If not, put your thinking cap on, because I'm not telling you. As it turned out, Harry had gotten a letter from his cousin Wolfgang who lived in Germany, telling him that he needed help. You see, Wolfgang was not that healthy since his bout with the mange. The chinchilla farm was getting a bit much for him to manage and so he required Harry's help in order to keep it running smooth. So, if you ever wondered about Harry's fate after the fairy tale, this is what happened to him. As far as I know, he liked it so much, he got his landed immigrant status and became a permanent resident of Germany. So, the three little pigs never had to worry about the big bad wolf again and life was quite peaceful for them now. Before their departure, Pinky told the twins that their good friend Peter Pan lived further down the yellow brick road. Should they run into him, to say hello from the three little pigs. The two agreed they would look him up when they arrived at Tinker-bell Village. You see, this is where Peter Pan lived. Realizing how late it was getting, the twins thought they should depart. Goodbyes were exchanged on both sides and Quick and Quack were finally on their way.

Dusk was beginning to set in just as the twins arrived at Tinkerbell Village. It was a sparkling residential area.

Everything twinkled here and so inviting! Quick and Quack went to the local coffee shop and asked the whereabouts of Peter Pan. They were told that he lived on a houseboat at the marina. Just turn right at the next stoplight and you can't miss it. And sure as anything, they found it. You definitely could not miss it! It was a huge ship with a sail and everything – just like in the story. What it actually was was Captain Hook's recycled ship. This tiny place was environmentally friendly. The residents here truly believed in recycling and sometimes to the extremes I might add. Let's face it, Captain Hook's ship! Now that's one for the books! Upon boarding the vessel, Peter Pan came out of the main cabin to greet them. He knew they were coming. Pinky had called him on his cell phone to inform Peter that they were friends of theirs and to treat them well. Remember the cell phone company (Zucchini Telecom), well; they had a monopoly throughout the forest. Big business always gets you, no matter where you live!! Peter was very nice to the twins. He offered them a place at his table for supper and a bed to sleep in- or rather two large nest boxes. Chickens don't sleep in beds, in case no one told you. If you didn't, you know it now. Amazing how educational a twisted story like this one can be. You see all the information you have acquired about giant chickens that you didn't know before! Peter introduced Quick and Quack to his new bride, Tinkerbell. They hadn't been married very long, only about six months. To them, the honeymoon was still ongoing. You know and I know, that won't last forever. It never does. But for now, the couple was very happy together. Coffee was served on the upper deck after a delicious meal. Tinkerbell was quite the chef in the kitchen. Eventually, the twins retired for the night, for they had a long journey ahead of them the next day. The pair slept very well on the houseboat that night. The sea was calm and quiet the whole time. They awoke to bright sunshine and brisk clean air. Due to the fact that everyone here was quite conscious of the environment, no pollution existed here or was allowed. After a good healthy breakfast, the two were on their way. Peter had told them to keep on the yellow brick road for about 3 chicken miles, then turn left at the sign saying: "Barney's Purple Dragon Inn ". If the twins turned to the right, they would end up in Dragon Alley. Peter had told them not to go there. Giant chickens were big, but nothing compared to dragons. And chickens were one of the dragon's favourite meals. Not to worry about meeting dragons along the way, for they were not allowed out of Dragon Alley. You see, when a dragon stepped out of Dragon Alley, he would turn into a crispy mini and end up on the assembly line at Nabisco. And no dragon wants that to happen! So long as the twins turned to the left, they were safe and no harm would come to them.

Now, you know how absent-minded kids are. If you ever had any, you would know!! It finally occurred to Quick and Quack that Cluck and Johephra- remember them; the parents- might be worried about them. So, on arriving at the sign Peter told them about, they went to the nearest payphone and called home to inform their parents that the pair were all right and would be home as soon as they figured out how to get out of the Enchanted Forest. You see, the twins had forgot their cell phone at home, so this is why a payphone had to be written into the story. Cluck and Johephra were delighted to hear from their offspring's. Upset yes, but not angry. They were so relieved to hear from them. It's a good thing the twins called when they did, because Cluck and Johephra were about to call in the Royal International Chicken Rangers to look for them. Wouldn't that have been something! Can you imagine that bunch going into the Enchanted Forest and the havoc they would have created? Let's not even go there.

After having made their all-important call, the twins set off for home. They weren't sure how long it would take them, so they couldn't give Cluck and Johephra a definite e.t.a. But Quick and Quack would be home before this story ends. This set their parents at ease for both knew this twisted tale could not last forever. The dynamic duo set off down the yellow brick road again. The yellow brick road was quite important in the Enchanted Forest. It was the only way in or out, let alone the fact that it was the only path in this magical kingdom. By the way, I forgot to mention, in case you haven't surmised it yet, this bright yellow road was a one-way route. One could only enter at the sign that said "ENTRANCE ' and leave through the ''EXIT''. You just had to pay attention to the notices along the way to end up at the correct destination. Now that you know all this, even you couldn't get lost. I hope I'm right about this. If not, you're in big trouble or you failed kindergarten –take your pick!!

Enough of this. As Quick and Quack went along their way, different characters seemed to pop up out of nowhere. First there was Rumplestiltskin (don't ask me how he got in this story), then Cinderella (she was running away from the prince - she found him a little too forward), Pinocchio (he got himself banished from wherever he lived for telling too many lies – his nose grew too big and there was no more room for him), and last but not least the infamous Puff the Magic Dragon. Where else would you find a magic dragon? Puff did not have to live in Dragon Alley because he was a good dragon. He didn't eat chickens. Like a good dragon should, his nourishment consisted of a balanced diet of vegetables, grain-fed meats, the proper amount of fiber and lots of milk. His secondary source of fluid was water. Dragon skin has to be kept moist so it stays soft and supple. This way it would not break when he flipped his tail around. His funds would not have to be spent on Oil Of Olay, L'Oreal, or Cover Girl products.

About late afternoon, Quick and Quack reached the famous "EXIT" sign. They had arrived at the end of the yellow brick road. Their journey had taken them to some fascinating places in a magical world of unicorns, snorks, talking walnuts, magic mushrooms and such. But now, it was time to get back to reality. As the twins headed for home – it was getting on to suppertime – they looked forward to one of Julia's delicious meals. After their evening meal, Quick and Quack would tell Cluck and Johephra of their incredible journey through the Enchanted Forest and all the great friends they had met there. Now, you tell me, have you ever had a journey like this one? If you had, please let me know what room you're in at the psych ward and I'll send you a box of chocolates.

We have come to the end of chapter 2. Stay tuned for more great adventures in the lives of our characters. This is like the never-ending story, but from a giant chickens point of view. By the way, in case you're wondering, this is still the tale of Jack And The Beanstalk. We will be hearing more about him in later in this series.

CHAPTER 3

If you recall, in chapter 2, our characters, Quick and Quack were leaving the Magic Forest and heading home just in time for one of Julia's scrumptious meals. Needless to say, upon their arrival, Cluck and Johephra were happy to see them, but a little upset that the two had ventured into the forest when they had been told not to. For now, Cluck and Johephra would listen to the pair tell of their incredible journey through the magic kingdom. Their parents were amazed at the amount of people living in the area. Long, long ago, Johephra had visited this place. At that time, it was scarcely populated. There were no villages or cities to be found. The only thing that he remembered distinctly was the yellow brick road. I guess since the road was put in, people had moved into the area to get away from the hustle and the bustle of the real world. Can't say as

I blame them! Have you noticed lately how insane the world is getting?

We will leave Quick and Quack behind for a while. Besides, they already had their adventure. It is now time for Daisy and Toronado. Their life at Southfork had gotten pretty hectic since Daisy won her academy award for best actress and Toronado seemed to be forever on the go between the United States and Spain. You've heard of bull flying through the air, well he was the real deal! It got so Twin Horn Airlines would always have a standing overseas ticket ready for him at all times. All this travelling was taking quite a toll on the poor bull. His black coat had started to turn a little grey. Now Toronado had to resort to "Just For Men" to keep up his appearances. After all, he had to look extremely presentable for the position he held. Black was Spain's favourite colour anyway. You've heard the saying "Once you go black you'll never go back ". It had never been truer than in this story for Toronado. And besides, with a looker like Daisy, he didn't want to take the chance of losing her to a younger bull. Between both their busy schedules, something had to give. And they definitely didn't want it to be their marriage. So the pair collaborated and decided to take a well-deserved vacation. The vacation had to be taken together. We want to keep them married in this tale. One divorce in a story is enough, don't you think? I know I ask you what you think about things once in a while, because, let's face it; you're the one reading the story.

Daisy and Toronado finally agreed on a caribbean cruise. The two had heard that Royal Caribbean Cruises offered very luxurious vacations. They thought this would be nice for a change. Neither had ever been on one, so this is what they did. Preparations were made to leave next month. May was a beautiful time of the year and they thought the weather would be just right for them. Daisy would make sure she packed everything that was required – sun tan lotion, hoof oil, electrolytes, udder cream (it's good for your complexion –dual purpose), Just for Men (Toronado still used it), and rubber shoes for dancing. It would be quite embarrassing should the pair slip and fall while on the dance floor. You see Daisy and Toronado were quite the dancers. Daisy had taken lessons for two years at Arthur Murray's School of Dance. She was very light on her feet for a bovine. Toronado was no slouch himself. He was a natural, being of Spanish descent and all. Even with her three-inch heels, she could two-step with the best of them. But the pair had their favourite. The bovine tango was their specialty. When Daisy and Toronado twirled, the room cleared – literally. You see, when you're that big, you need a lot of space. Could you see them tango in a nine by twelve? It just wouldn't work! Well, I guess we had better get on with the story.

Everyone from Southfork was there to see them off. Jack, Mildred, the children one through twelve, Cluck, Johephra, Quick and Quack, Ophillia and Bernard. Even Billy-Bob showed up. He assured the two that he would look after their affairs while they were gone. Toronado had taken a leave of absence for the amount of time required, and Daisy had even turned down a leading role in the upcoming movie "The Cow Jumped Over The Moon". Their time together was more important. Little did they know what they were in for!

The ship they boarded, the U.S.S. Bullfrog, was a beautiful vessel. Luxury was at its peak here. No expense was spared when this sucker was built. Staterooms were large and spacious and even had a balcony with marble troughs so passengers could breakfast or supper outdoors in the brisk clean air should they choose to do so. Attendance was not required in the formal dining room. Being the celebrities they were, the couple chose to stay away from the crowds. After all, this was their time. With the crew that lived at Southfork, you didn't have a whole lot of time to be together and fool around. You just try to have a good time with that many kids and chickens running all over the place! Quickies are fine once in a while, but, as you know, the whole package is definitely BETTER!!!

After a few days in their overly large stateroom – remember we talked about this, a cow and a bull can't exactly live in a closet – it was time to get out and take a tour of the ship. Besides, the pair was getting a little worn out. Need I say more! If I have to, someone should tell you the tale of the birds and the bees and I advise an appointment with Dr. Phil.

At this same time in fairy tale history, there was a buccaneer named Blackbeard. I think you've heard of him. He was pretty famous in his day. Now Blackbeard decided that his tale was getting a little mundane, so he proceeded to escape his imaginary world and step into reality. Besides that, reality was one place he had never been before. Once there he must secure a vessel. If you recall, he was a pirate's ship captain and that was the only formal training he had. So, in staying true to his nature, he hijacked a Cuban gunboat – it was the only one he could find at the time – threw everyone overboard (gave them life jackets- he did have a bit of a soft spot when he wanted to), gathered up his crew and sailed away. It didn't take long before his band of swashbucklers figured out how to operate the ship. They were a very observant bunch. You pretty well have to when your trade is piracy. Now, as everyone knows, pirates do like to take a little drink now and then. So the crew headed to the nearest L.C.B.O. for their supplies. Once there, they were astonished at the variety to choose from. The only thing that upset Blackbeard some was the fact that his friend Captain Morgan had made the label, and not him in this world of reality. Once the supplies were loaded, Blackbeard headed for warmer waters. He knew the Caribbean well – from his former fairy tale – so guess where they headed!

Now, we know that Daisy and Toronado were on a Caribbean cruise, kind of like a second honeymoon, but now we have Blackbeard in the picture. And you know he'll definitely mess this up for them. After all, if he didn't our adventure for the pair would be lost. So, here goes.

As it happened, both ships were on the same course, without either one's knowledge. Can you imagine the look on their faces, when, on rounding the Rock Of Gibraltar, the Royal Caribbean cruise ship, the U.S.S. Bullfrog, came face to face with Blackbeard's Cuban gunboat flying the skull and crossbones. Wouldn't that blow your mind!! I don't know about you, but it would do a number on mine. The swashbuckling pirate being who he was, did what came naturally to him. He and his crew boarded the Bullfrog and seized her as his own. One does not argue with a loaded gunboat. All passengers were called to the upper deck for inspection by Blackbeard. He wasn't quite sure about all this new-fangled modern stuff, but he would adjust. This vessel was a little large for his liking, so he proceeded to take what he wanted and leave the rest. Like I told you, he had mellowed in his old age, so he didn't wipe everyone out. Out of the corner of his eye, he spotted Daisy. She was a real fox, he thought, for a bovine. So, Daisy went to the top of his I want list. She was not impressed. He wasn't exactly Valentino. Far from it she thought. Pretty homely even for a human. If she was to be captured, at least he could be good looking. But she's not the one writing this story, is she? Toronado was baffled on what to do to get his beloved out of this situation. He thought and thought and then it came to him.

Sneaking away through the side stairwell, he lowered a lifeboat to the water – it wasn't hard, it was an inflatable one – secured a motor and waited for the right moment. He would follow the gunboat to their destination and rescue Daisy. Along with him, he took his trusty dueling sword, just in case. Toronado was somewhat of an artist when it came to fencing. To keep silent and incognito while following the gunboat, he tied up alongside on their blind spot, so as to avoid detection. It worked very well actually. Just before arriving at Taratoga on the island of Maltese (that's where the falcon lived) Toronado untied from the vessel and snuck ashore. Here he waited till the moment was just right. Blackbeard had tied Daisy to a tree nearby and he and his crew left to do lunch. On seeing this, Toronado rushed over to Daisy, untied her, and both hurried to the lifeboat he had left harbored in the bushes. What the pair did not know was that Blackbeard and his band of thieves were doing a quick lunch, not an afternoon siesta. On hearing the sound of the engine from the lifeboat, Blackbeard turned to see his precious booty being taken from him. That's what he called Daisy. Don't worry, she wasn't impressed either! He rushed to his ship and called for his crew, who, for some reason were not responding. What Blackbeard did not know was that the band of buccaneers had forgot to bring their supply of gravol with them. It had been a long time since they had been on the high seas and they hadn't had time to acclimatize themselves with this new world. This gave Daisy and Toronado time to get a good head start. And the two wasted no time in doing so. The little lifeboat sped across the water likety split. Not far ahead stood a group of islands. This seemed like the logical place to go. What lay before them, they did not know, but it had to be better than Blackbeard and his bunch. When Toronado looked back, he could see the gunboat in the distance and heading straight for them. All of a sudden the ship stopped. This seemed very strange. You'll find out shortly and wonder why you didn't think of it. Now, remember, logic plays no part in this tale, so if you are as twisted as I think you may be, you will not have a problem with the answer.

If you thought things were a bit strange before, just wait! The islands that Toronado and Daisy had come upon were very special ones. They had landed on Fairy Island –the metropolis of the kingdom of fairies. I'll bet you didn't see that coming! When the characters from the movie "Voyage of the Unicorn" were let go, their contract stated that a permanent residence would be provided to them. This is where Fairy Island comes into the picture. Now, you know we had to keep with the program, so magic ultimately has to play a part in here somewhere. Why not here? It seems logical. Molaki, the island's great soothsayer and his sidekick Sebastian met Daisy and Toronado at the peer. They were impressed. It's not in every imaginary story that you get to meet these two world wonders. Molaki was a medium sized wizard, as wizard's go, but extremely vivid. His partner,

Sebastian, was smaller in stature, but just as colorful. When asked why the ship had stopped dead in its tracks on the high seas, Molaki explained to the pair that an invisible force field protected the kingdom. By the way, that was also part of the settlement when their contract with the movie studio expired. So, all worries were laid to rest and the honeymooners may as well enjoy their vacation as best they could.

Molaki had arranged for a carriage to pick up the couple and take them to their temporary residence while on Fairy Island. It wasn't hard. Even here they had cell phones. He would see them later. When their transportation arrived, Daisy and Toronado could not believe their eyes. Daisy was sure she had seen this carriage before somewhere. It would come to her, she thought. Just give me time. Finally, it came to her. This was the same one she had read about in the book "Cinderella ". If it wasn't, it sure looked the same. Well, you guessed it. It was the same one. When Cinderella's fairy tale ended, they weren't quite sure what to do with all the props. So, being capitalistic, as humans are, for the most part, the company held an auction and sold off all the items they had no need for anymore. The crew that settled on Fairy Island decided this carriage would fit beautifully in their new surroundings. So, this is how Cinderella's buggy came to be on Fairy Island. I'll bet that's a new one for you! The only difference was that three blind mice, not six white horses, were pulling it. The mice, Eeny, Minee, and Moe had vision problems, but were not really blind. They all wore special contact lenses that gave them twenty twenty vision. So, you see, it was not the blind leading the blind!

The scenery on their way to the suite arranged for them at Fantasy Island Hotel, which had a five star rating according "Better Hotels and Gardens", was absolutely breathtaking. Flowers of every colour and shape lined the yellow brick road. Yes, I said the yellow brick road. You're not seeing things. I'll explain this a little later. Gardens were lush with pink gardenias, vanilla scented white roses, vibrant blue and red hydrangeas, soft lilac wisteria, every flower imaginable was here. Daisy and Toronado had never seen so much beauty in all their bovine lives. Bush Gardens didn't even come close to this place! The couple noticed the trees were a bit odd here. All the trunks were smooth, with limbs impeccably placed with such care and perfection. It was just amazing! The buggy ride was something one could only dream about, and smooth too. You see, the wheels on the carriage were of the best quality – Michelin super tires, extra large of course. They had been ordered on e-bay special for this purpose. And Super Stork Express had delivered them just in time it seemed. Well, on with our tour.

Upon arriving at the hotel, the two were led up to their suite by O'Reilly. Now, O'Reilly was small in comparison to most, a little on the green side – as far as complexion goes – with the pointiest ears the two had ever seen. He looked an awful lot like a leprechaun.

That's because he was one. He had come to be here when the battle between the little people and the mini-druids had broke out. O'Reilly was not into violence in any way, shape or form, so he decided to leave Ireland and head for new horizons. He had read the brochure on Fairy Island and thought this was just the place for him. Of course, finding the right airline to take him there was not easy. Booking had to be done well in advance, for seats were limited to this destination. When was the last time you tried to fly to Fairy Island? See what I mean! This little fellow blended right in. With all the fabulous colour here, he would not be out of place or different. Maybe a touch smaller, but that was a minor detail he could live with.

Now back to Toronado and Daisy. You will notice that Toronado was mentioned before Daisy here. I thought it was about time Toronado got top billing for a change. Daisy didn't mind. She thought he was hot stuff anyway. This was definitely a top-notch resort. Marble floors, ornate cathedral ceilings, magnificent spiral staircases, the softest plush carpeting, nothing was left to chance. The hallways were wide and spacious. Toronado and Daisy had no problems here. Lots of room and superb surroundings. What else could one ask for? This place made "Tara "-you know the plantation from Gone With The Wind – look like the ghetto. Even the old Donald would be grateful to have reservations at this spread.

When the couple arrived at their room, the grandeur continued. Double doors opened onto the largest room the two had ever seen. The furniture was of the best that could be found and let me tell you, when you live in the imagination, you would be surprised at what you can create. Anything is possible. You should know that by now. A spacious kitchen was also provided, should Daisy want to try her hand at the culinary arts. Not that she did much of that at Southfork. With the busy schedule she had, time in the kitchen was a luxury for her. Don't kid yourself, Daisy enjoyed cooking and such things, but when you're a star, time to oneself is somewhat of a rarity. Anyhow, back to our story. The view from the enormous circular balcony was a feast for the eyes to behold. You could see for miles. The beauty of this land was beyond compare. No wonder this place was so booked. Everyone who was anyone in the fairy tale world came here to holiday. Who could blame them!

After a good night's rest, Toronado and Daisy awoke to a delicious breakfast of the best triple clean oats and hay that one could desire. A leisurely stroll through the magnificent gardens and a romantic walk along the beach seemed just what the two needed. After all, this was their holiday. The waters here were a crystal sapphire blue and the sand on the beach felt good under their hooves. If only this could last forever. But not so, or our adventure with these two bovine would be over way too soon. And we can't let that happen, can we?

On arriving back at the hotel, Molaki was waiting for them. He hadn't been waiting long, so he was still in a good mood. Never make a wizard wait for any length of time. Their capabilities, should one irritate them, could be endless. We can't have that happen, for then our story would be never-ending. And that is just not acceptable. Molaki, and his trusty companion, Sebastian, told Toronado and Daisy of all the sights to see on the island. They had only to follow the yellow brick road, and it would take them anywhere they wished to go. Now, you remember earlier in this story, I said I would tell you of the yellow brick road being here. Well, now is the time.

If you recall, from chapter 2, this legendary highway was located in the "Magic Forest ". What I didn't tell you about was the underground tunnel that existed between these two places. When the construction industry was at its peak and fairy dollars were abundant throughout, the King and Queen of Fairy Island decided to invest in their kingdom's future. They realized that tourism was going to be really big, so a way to the island had to be made possible. What better way to do this than a tunnel? Not just any tunnel at that either. This thoroughfare would be spacious, with wide pathways on either side for those who felt energetic enough to hike it, and soundproof - no echoing here –the walls of this tunnel being well padded. The padding would also ensure that anyone driving over here, in case of a mishap or not having his or her drivers' license would not be hurt. However, there was a small toll fee to be paid to travel this road. As you already know, from living in the real world, road maintenance is not cheap, no matter where you live. Since the two islands were similar in lifestyle, as far as fantasy goes, the C.E.O.'s of each area held a meeting, with permission from their board of directors of course, and agreed on the construction of the underground causeway. So, now you know how the yellow brick road made it all the way to Fairy Island. Now wasn't that an interesting fact that no one told you about when you were reading the Wizard Of Oz. Well, the secret is out now, with their consent, of course. The next time you are planning a vacation, maybe, instead of Disneyland, you should check out Fairy Island and all that it has to offer. It's in their brochure should you be lucky enough to find one.

Daisy and Toronado lunched out on the main patio of the hotel and afterwards settled down for an afternoon rest in their suite. The couple would venture out later on in the day. When they awoke, the two felt refreshed and decided it was time to check out more of the island. On following one of the many paths that led away from the hotel - by the way, these were what you would call "off the beaten path ", not the yellow brick road - the pair came upon a very strange sight. Coconuts were growing out of the ground, lining each side of the path. These coconuts were extremely large. Toronado and Daisy couldn't even see over them. This must be the famous Coconut Grove that everyone was talking about, Daisy thought. The bovine duo were pretty impressed. In all their fame and fortune, they had never had time to visit such a place. Schedules wouldn't allow it. Now Daisy could say she was at the Coconut Grove and impress all her friends. She could be a little vain at times. Not too often though. As the two passed through the grove, they came upon a small clearing. In the center of this clearing was an enormous tree with full limbs that reached beyond the clouds. This was quite the phenomenon. Such a huge tree all by it's lonesome. The two looked around and were baffled by this. Had the pair seen the sign to the right, they would have known this was the famous Tree of Knowledge. Daisy and Toronado were astounded when Tree spoke to them with such overwhelming confidence. We'll call him Tree in this tale. If you can come up with something better, please let me know. I would love to hear it. Tree greeted the couple with the normal chit-chat that people usually say, touching on the weather, their stay here and such. Daisy and Toronado had heard of this famous tree, but did not know that it actually existed. They did now! And so do you. Aren't you the lucky one!

Daisy asked Tree of her future and things to come. Toronado also had a lot of questions for it. We are using the term it, so as not to offend any one gender. This way, no one can say this story is biased. To their surprise, Tree could not give them an answer. You see, it was a tree of knowledge. It knew a lot of stuff, but not the future. How could it? The future hadn't happened yet. Anyway, after a lengthy conversation with Tree, the two were on their way. The one thing that Tree did tell them about was to beware of the triads. They could be a sneaky lot sometimes. Now, if you have never heard of a triad, it is a tree spirit that lives in the forests of magical places. As you pass through their domain, the triads slither about through the limbs of the giant conifers whispering strange secrets to those who wish to hear. Only those who believed could see them.

Being on the off beaten path, Daisy and Toronado knew anything could happen on this little escapade. Whatever occurred, they would deal with it in their own diplomatic style. That's one thing the pair were really good at, diplomacy. After passing through the clearing and saying their goodbyes to Tree, the couple noticed a fairly large sign directly ahead of them. This sign read "Welcome All Visitors, You Are Now Entering The Land of The Triad – Population 340 and Possibly Growing ". Toronado thought this should be a good one! What else could they come up with in this absolutely insane story?

The forest here was different than any other. Trunks were soft and supple, swaying in the warm breeze, the branches acting as giant fans keeping the temperature just right. You see, temperature control was a major factor for the triads. It could not reach more than 75 degrees and no less than 68.32. Should the span go beyond this, triads would dissolve and fade away. They were wispy creatures resembling humans, but transparent as if ghosts. All wore laurels as their headdress and luxurious sheer togas purchased from Victoria Secret. The catalogue has angels, doesn't it, so it would seem logical that it be written into this tale. Pale in complexion - you would be pale too if you were a ghost – with deep blue eyes that glowed in the dark, the triads meandered through the forest, winding up and down trees in every direction imaginable. Daisy and Toronado – we're back to Daisy having top billing, Toronado wasn't comfortable with the change - could hear endless whispering throughout. You see, they believed, so the couple could hear. It told of secrets that fairy tale history had never divulged. And we mustn't either. It would be against triad law. Every community has to have a law and this was theirs. Daisy and Toronado followed the winding path till they came to a large cavern entrance. Not far into the entrance of the cave, the two could see sparkling lights. As they entered this place, a whole new world opened up to them. Amazing lights lit the corridors and hallways, stars seemingly suspended in mid air and shining like diamonds. At the main entrance further down were large oval doors made of pale blue crystallite. Daisy and Toronado didn't realize they were only in the foyer of the great cavern. Every once in a while a triad would wisp up to them and give directions as to the accepted protocol here. These triads wore aquamarine togas. All triads, after completing their elementary education, were obliged to take an internship for 2 years. Once completed, they were issued the aquamarine gown on their graduation. The graduating triads were now considered to be in the upper echelon of their society. From there, they would proceed to the cavern to serve the King and Queen. The couple graciously accepted their advice and kept on. This long corridor eventually led up to the sacred chamber. A nymph on either side guarded the chamber; each bearing a gold saber ornately inlayed with rubies and saphires that glimmered in the light of the stars. Because they believed, Daisy and Toronado were allowed to enter the great room. The nymphs opened the doors to reveal a spectacle never seen before.

The room was enormous with walls of gold, and jade statues of Venus De Milo filling each corner. I assume you realize the room was square or it would not have corners. If you hadn't, we'd better have a talk. You may have some serious problems that you are not aware of and that's as far as I'll go on that one. In the center of the room were two thrones of regal stature. It was on these thrones that Daisy and Toronado met King Alberto and Queen Fiona. Alberto and Fiona were the rulers of Fairy Island. After formal introductions, the royal couple invited the honeymooners for a hot cup of chamomile tea. This was their beverage of choice. Fiona informed Daisy that it relaxed her and seem to relieve all the stress of running a kingdom. The two couples conversed and told of each other's lives together.

As it turned out, Alberto was of royal descent. Fiona was not. The king had met her while on a field trip in Tucson, Arizona with the graduate students of Fairy University. You see, Alberto liked to be involved with his people so as to enable him to be a good ruler. Fiona was a cocktail waitress in one of the local bars there. When the two met, it was love at first sight. To get approval from his peers, Alberto sent Fiona to Royal Protocol School. This had better work thought Alberto or he would have to take a job as a bartender in Tucson. Well, it did and the two still live happily in this surreal world to this day. Daisy and Toronado were glad it did for them. They were such nice people for fairies and all. It was getting late and our adventurers had to get back to their hotel. Molaki had arranged a dinner for the four that evening. Now, the last thing you want to do is tick a wizard off. So, Daisy and Toronado said their goodbyes and headed back to their suite. Getting lost on the way to the hotel was no consequence. Alberto and Fiona had left specific orders for guides to accompany the couple out of the Land Of The Triads.

Daisy and Toronado arrived back at their suite with time to spare. After all, they must dress for dinner. Daisy looked absolutely stunning in her yellow organza gown. It really brought out her skin tone. She was of the limousine line, so yellow truly suited her. Toronado wore his black tuxedo. Black was his colour of choice you know. Talk about being colour co coordinated. These two were a fashion statement in itself! Molaki and Sebastian were waiting for them in the main dining room when they arrived. The four discussed the events of the day and to Daisy and Toronado's surprise discovered that Fiona once lived in a small shoe not far from where Mildred, remember Jack's wife, used to reside. At that time in reality, there weren't too many shoes available so it seemed to Daisy that this was a little more than a coincidence. She turned out to be right, as women usually are, about Fiona. She really was Mildred's second cousin through marriage. Talk about a small world. Daisy would have to get in touch with Fiona when she got back and inform her of the discovery. Maybe the royal couple could visit them at Southfork some day.

Mildred would be so happy to see her. Daisy would e-mail her when she returned home. The bovine couple had no time to go back and see them. They had to catch the ferry to the mainland the next morning. The yellow brick road only connected Fairy Island to the Magic Forest. And this is not where Daisy and Toronado were headed. Before they left, Molaki gave the couple Fiona's e-mail address – *Fionafairy@space.xl*. Let's face it; even you would remember this address. I know I would!

After a good night's sleep, Daisy and Toronado were up early to meet the ferry. Ahab, the ship's captain greeted them on arrival. The weather channel had fore-casted a beautiful sunny day with no bad weather in sight. The pair were looking forward to a smooth trip to the mainland. Seas were calm, winds were soft, this should be smooth sailing. Or so it would seem. But, remember, this is a twisted tale, not your ordinary run of the mill story. You know something has to go wrong. And it did!

About two hours into the trip a storm arose. The seas were vicious, winds whipping at the small ferry and tossing her about from side to side. Everyone on board was directed to put on their flotation devices, just in case they had to jump ship. Amazing through all of this there were no mishaps. A few passengers shook up a little, but nothing serious. It's a good thing Daisy had remembered to bring her gravol along, not like some buccaneers we know! When the storm subsided, Ahab found his ferry grounded on a reef. Not far from this spot, Daisy, Toronado, and Ahab could see land in the distance. With land in sight, all were relieved to know that they would not be stuck in this surreal tale forever. This madness must end sometime they thought. If you were in this story, wouldn't you want it to end?

Ahab looked out to see four small vessels approaching the ferry. He thought this a bit strange. On taking a closer look, he noticed that these miniature speedboats were being driven by rabbits. There seemed to be one larger than the rest who was giving direction to the others. This had to be the head honcho. The ferry's captain thought these tiny vessels would never be able to free his ship. Little did he know these same boats were powered by twin diesel engines. Bringing the ferry into port was no problem for them.

I know you're wondering about the rabbit thing. At this point in the story, I cannot keep it a secret any longer. In order for this tale to go on, I must tell you why these rabbits and this place are so important. The following will explain everything. The ferry had run aground just off Bunny Hop Island. Only rabbits lived here. These were not your run of the mill rabbits and this was no ordinary island. It was the birthplace of Peter Rabbit. Here, all rabbits were highly educated. Some had their masters degree, some their doctorate, some just good old professors of rabbit language. In the world of Peter Rabbit, and by the way, no one knows this till now, was a school of the highest caliber, Hop University. It even beat out Harvard and Oxford in the International School Rating System. This, Daisy and Toronado had to see! So, as usual, on their way they went. The sun always shone here, skies were always blue, and crystal clear waters flowed through the sparkling streams. The underbrush was like a carpet of velvet under their hooves. This must be rabbit heaven. Daisy didn't realize how right she was. What no one knew before this story was that there actually is a rabbit heaven. When their fairy tales came to an end, all rabbits were instructed to go to downloads and would automatically be transferred here. Now you know how Bunny Hop Island came to be. Didn't you always want to know this? I know I did and so should you.

This is where Peter Rabbit had retired. Actually, he didn't have much of a choice, did he? Anyway, on with our story. Peter was an ambitious and very industrious rabbit. He went into agriculture in a big way. Carrots were his main produce. From here, he created health juices, carrot cakes and muffins. They were in such great demand that in order to fill the supply, he opened a chain of bakeries all over the world. These products, of course, must be exported from Fairy Island. Peter solved that problem by developing a shipping company called "Quick As A Bunny". This seems pretty logical to me, don't you think? Of course, logic doesn't necessarily play a big part in this story.

Now, Peter wasn't satisfied with only one endeavor. He had heard through the grapevine that Easter was a big holiday for humans. After thoroughly researching this fact, he had an amazing idea. So, Peter being who he was followed through. Every other venture had been successful, why not this one. He needed the right location for this and found Easter Island to be ideal. Here he built a chocolate egg factory to meet the demand for this special holiday. Because of the fact that he was so busy at home, he went into partnership with the Lindy Hop Chocolate Co. Now, are you starting to catch on to the importance in history of Bunny Hop Island? If not, you have never read Mother Goose and it's about time you did. The investment turned out to be extremely profitable for both. Every year, at the same time in reality, millions of chocolate eggs are shipped out and sold throughout the universe. It would take a whole chicken year to produce enough eggs to fill the growing demand. This also kept unemployment at an all time low on Bunny Hop Island. Our government should take a lesson from this. But, they won't. You tell me when they have ever listened to anyone but themselves. If you can, you must be a politician and I wouldn't tell anyone if I were you. Keep it a secret, you may last longer! Easter is still celebrated and Peter and his business partners are still in production to this day. I know I haven't mentioned the Easter Bunny as of yet. There is a reason for this omission in chapter 3. You will learn Easter Bunny's fate in chapter 4 and just maybe, you will find out this isn't such a fairy tale after all!!

Don't worry, we haven't forgotten about Daisy and Toronado. I know we still have to get them back home. And we will, so not to worry.

It was getting on lunchtime, so Peter offered sustenance for everyone on board. If they didn't like carrot cakes or muffins, or if they had any allergies to them, they were out of luck. It couldn't be helped. After all, they were on Bunny Hop Island. To everyone's delight, the muffins and cakes filled their empty stomachs and left all well satisfied. It was now time to depart. All alien life forms were allowed to visit the island, but no other species but rabbits were allowed to stay, even for one night. Remember how I told you every community had a law, well; this was Bunny Hop Island's. There are no criminals in this story and we are not about to start letting them in. I know Blackbeard is here, but he isn't really a criminal, just a pirate bored with his fairy tale.

All proceeded down to the peer to board the ferry. Ahab and the passengers thanked Peter and his friends for their hospitality, and then set sail for home. Peter had given Ahab a map that would take him to his destination in order that the little ferry not get lost. You'd want a map too if you were in this story!!

No storm was in sight. The local bunny channel had predicted a bright sunny day with calm seas. We know this one will be right. It was the bunny channel after all, and bunnies were never wrong. The little vessel sailed along with no mishaps whatsoever. Wasn't this a nice change for them! They were all so pleased about it, they sent an e-mail thanking me. It does feel good to be appreciated even if it is fairy tale characters.

Peter had given Ahab the exact co-ordinates of the U.S.S. Bullfrog. He had had a state of the art tracking system installed in the watch house on Bunny Hop Island. You see, Peter just knew, that in this story, someone would escape his or her fairy tale. So, to be on the safe side, he ordered the best that bunny dollars could buy. He wasn't sure when it would happen, but he knew it would. I wonder if Peter is a psychic in disguise, or he read this story somewhere else and didn't tell us? I am almost positive it was option one because no one in their right mind would even think of writing this stuff!

Ahab followed the directions given to a tee and sure enough, there she was. Still intact and not a mark on her, the Bullfrog was waiting for them. Unknown to them, the cruise ship had been equipped with a very sophisticated computer system with an auto microchip program. It was set up so that should any passengers that were micro chipped get lost, the vessel would stop and wait for their return. Of course, all who boarded the Bullfrog were automatically micro chipped. It was one of the shipping rules in this part of the world. This is why the Bullfrog had such an unblemished record when it came to "lost passengers". Daisy and Toronado could finally finish what they started – their cruise. The couple found their journey quite interesting, but after everything that had happened, Southfork was looking pretty darn good to them!

Well, they finally did reach homeport and were glad of it. Everyone was present to greet the couple - Jack, Mildred, the children one through twelve inclusive, Cluck, Johephra, Quick and Quack, Ophillia, Bernard and we mustn't forget Billy-Bob. It sure was great to be home again. Everyone piled into the stretch limo and headed for Southfork. On arrival, all the families gathered in the great room to hear of the fantastic voyage Daisy and Toronado had taken. Neither of the two seemed none the worse for wear. Even with all the mishaps, Daisy and Toronado looked refreshed and suntanned. The trip had done them both good and now they were ready to resume their careers. The couple would take a few days to relax, then it would be back to work we go!

If you wondered whatever happened to Ahab, he left the ferry business and took an apprenticeship with Royal Caribbean Cruise Lines. If you should happen to run into him on your next cruise, say hello to him for me and tell him the crew at Southfork says "hi" and will never forget what he did for them. We will leave our characters now and let them enjoy some peace and quiet – at least as much as they can with all those children and chickens running around. By the way, they all say hello and hope to see you in chapter 4.

CHAPTER 4

On leaving chapter 3, Daisy and Toronado had just returned from their fantastic voyage into fairyland and Ahab had gone to work for Royal Caribbean cruise lines. By the way, did you run into Ahab on your cruise? Please let me know how he is doing. I haven't seen him since chapter 3. I think he'll do just fine, after all he was a pretty smart cookie.

A year later in our story, Jack and Mildred decided it was time to visit Mildred's long lost cousin Fiona. Remember her, the Queen of Fairy Island? Ophellia and Bernard, who had married by now, would take care of the children one through twelve inclusive while the two went on vacation. They also had Big Bird to help them, so it should be pretty smooth sailing. Let's face it, if you had twelve kids, you'd need a vacation too! The couple had booked their tickets well in advance, for seats were quite limited to this part of the world.

I have told you this before, but I thought a reminder might be in order. The airline of choice was "Chicken Wings Express". Jack got a real deal here for it was one of Johephra's subsidiary companies. Along the way, they were to have a stop over in Australia, where Jack's cousin, from Ophellia's first marriage, lived. He hadn't seen her for quite some time. And when we're talking fairy tales, that's eons.

You know her as Little Bo Peep. Actually, she married, but kept her maiden name, since everyone in the fairy tale hall of fame knew her as "Little Bo Peep ". She had a thriving sheep business just outside of Sydney, Australia raising counting sheep for the Serta Posture-pedic Company. It was a very lucrative business since the technical media explosion. The mattress market had soared in the last few years. Just to keep up with supply and demand, Peep had to keep a minimum count of at least 5,000 sheep. And that's a lot of sheep for one little girl to maintain. Every day, she would go out, with her trusty companion Acronis, and take roll call. You see, Acronis was always present when this was done for he was her backup system in case of an error. This pretty well looked after her day. Even though they all wore numbers, it was still quite a feat to count them all. But Peep didn't mind the work. She thoroughly enjoyed the fresh air – she was a country girl – and loved her sheep dearly. She was extremely proud of their success.

Jack had e-mailed Little Bo Peep to let her know that he and his wife would be arriving in Sydney on flight 222 at approximately 3:00 p.m. June 21. Peep was thrilled to get the news, for she hadn't seen Jack in years. The last time they had seen each other; he was only 3 years old. My goodness, time really does fly even in fairy tales! Peep was anxious to show off her counting sheep. After all, if it weren't for them, she would not be the success she is today. Instructions were given to the staff at "Mutton 123" to prepare the guesthouse and make sure that nothing but the best was put out. Linens for the bed were of the finest Egyptian cotton, the best bone china was taken out of storage, and the most fragrant of flowers were placed in crystal vases throughout the cottage. To make sure everything was perfect, Peep had hired Steven and Chris (you know them as the Designer Guys) , who happened to be vacationing in the area at the time, to come and inspect Jack and Mildred's residence since they were staying not far from Mutton 123. All seemed to be in order other than a few minor details, which promptly got sorted out. Peep was as ready as she would ever be for her guests.

In order for Peep to have the time to entertain, a temporary staff must be hired. After all, one cannot entertain and count sheep at the same time. It just doesn't work. Especially when you have that many! An advertisement was placed in the local newspaper in Sydney requesting the need for domestic engineers – temporary of course. Well, To Peep's surprise, she hit the jackpot. You won't believe who applied for the job! It was, you guessed it, none other than Mary Poppins.

Who could have asked for more! Mary had been in between jobs, and this was right up her alley. She was not as young as she used to be. Umbrella hoping and children were a little too stressful for her now. Peep also had to hire a sheep counter. Lucky for her, Australia's best was available –Digits Mcphee. Everything was perfect, or so it seemed, for now. Don't worry, disaster will come, but not till later. Let's get Jack and Mildred there first.

The couple arrived on schedule, due to the fact that "Chicken Wings Express" was a very prompt airline. Now, isn't that a switch! Have you ever seen an airline on time? The last time I checked, it had been quite a while since that happened. Peep met Jack and Mildred at the terminal and all proceeded to the lounge for refreshments. They had a lot of catching up to do. And a good stiff drink wouldn't hurt either after such a long flight. They chatted and caught up on all the news from each other's lives. Peep was astounded at the progression of events that had brought Jack and his family to South-fork. Ever since her fairy tale, Peep had always lived at Mutton 123. Our gracious hostess had arranged for a limousine to take them back the ranch. The scenery on the way was fabulous. It was not at all what Jack and Mildred had pictured. The brochures of Australia had not done it justice. Mutton 123 wasn't that much out of the way, only about a two-hour ride. On arrival, the visiting couple was quite impressed. Peep's home was large with a west wing and an east wing. To the left of the mansion, a mutton - shaped pool awaited all who wished a relief from the heat that sometimes plagued the area. Just off the pool stood a refreshment bar with a gazebo. Unknown to most, Little Bo Peep could be quite the partier when she wanted to. It wasn't often, but when she did, watch out! The cottage had been built behind the main house with a cobblestone path leading to the entrance of the mansion. All in all, it was somewhat like Southfork, but in Australia.

The cottage couldn't have been more perfect. Being away from the main house, it gave Jack and Mildred the time they so desperately needed for themselves. This was something that was hard to find at Southfork with the children and all. Don't get me wrong, Jack and Mildred loved the children one through twelve inclusive very much, but their personal time together was very limited. Once settled in the quaint residence at Mutton 123, the couple proceeded to the main house for a nightcap with their host. This lasted for about an hour or so, and then Jack and Mildred said their goodnight and retired to the cottage for the remainder of the evening. They were exhausted after the long trip and tomorrow would be big day.

Now, you have to realize this sheep ranch consisted of 10,000 acres, the majority being prime farmland. After all, if you're going to raise 5,000 sheep you need a plenty of room. They may not be as big as giant chickens, but they're sure were a whole mess of them. I must tell you, even on the best of farms, there are good lands and there are Bad Lands. Mutton 123 had a lot of one and a bit of the other. Another fact that I forgot to mention is that Peep had donated an entire section of her property to animal wildlife preserve. This is where Skippy the kangaroo and his gang lived. In another section lived the giant hares. I know I told you rabbits automatically went to downloads after their fairy tale ended, but these were hares and giant ones at that, not fairy tale rabbits. There is a difference you know! Size alone would tell you that. If not, we have a problem and it isn't mine, believe me! On one section of the badlands were caves and caverns, some of which went deep into the ground. No one had actually explored these, so they were virtually unknown territory. With all those sheep to count, Peep hadn't had the time. Now that you have a general layout of Mutton 123, we can go on with our story.

The next morning bright and early, everyone met for breakfast on the patio of the main house. It was delicious. Mary Poppins had outdone herself. Fresh crescent rolls, luscious strawberries, mangos, pineapple, toasted coconuts (special import from the Coconut Grove), and of course eggs benedict adorned the table for her guests. It was a feast fit for a king. All indulged to their hearts content and after all appetites were satisfied, retired to their rooms to prepare for the day's journey.

Peep had the chauffeur bring the Landrover Deluxe around to the front entrance. If you're going to entertain, you may as well do it right. And Peep knew how to do just that. She had also instructed Mary to prepare a picnic lunch and refreshments for the day trip. The Landrover pulled out of the drive and headed toward the northeast section where the counting sheep were grazing lazily on the rich pasture. What else would they be doing out there? The counting sheep weren't very good at hide and seek, possibly because there were very few trees or they just didn't know how to play the game. I'm afraid the only formal training they had consisted of being counted. At this, they were quite ambitious. You see, these were very serious sheep. On arriving, Jack and Mildred were impressed. All the numbers were in order and so very meticulously placed. Absolutely nothing was out of alignment. Peep sure ran a tight ship! Digit was up in the watch house keeping an eye on things, with Acronis at his side. Even though Digit was one of the best counters, Peep required that Acronis be there at all times. After all he was her back up system. Should anything go wrong, Acronis could bring it up, locate the error, and do the correction. All in all, it was a pretty sure fire system. Almost!! And you know what that means – something is coming, but I won't tell you now. You'll have to read the rest of the story to find out.

Our crew of adventurers then headed south to check out another section the ranch. Here, things looked quite different. The soil was red, with small trees popping up here and there. On one side of the valley, a stream meandered through the crevices in the boulders that lined it. A little bit on the odd side, but then, we're in Australia if you remember. If you've never been there, I could say anything. If you have, well, it is a fairy tale, isn't it? This is where Hoppy and his band of giant hares lived. Hoppy considered this his personal territory. The sign he had posted stated as much. It read the following: "Hoppy's Giant Hare Reserve ". The sign also gave instructions to all visitors to proceed to checkpoint Charlie for inspection upon arrival. You see, a pass had to be issued in order for the visitors to go on with their tour. Hoppy liked to keep track of the entire goings on in his area. He was very meticulous this way. So our crew did what was required of them, were issued day passes, and went on with their journey. Peep didn't mind this set up at all. This way, she had no worries concerning intruders on the property. Hoppy looked after this end with absolute precision. A few miles later, the vehicle stopped and all its' passengers disembarked. They had come to a beautiful meadow where flowers bloomed, eucalyptus trees gave shade, and a pool of crystal clear water refreshed the air. It was the perfect place for a picnic. Peep's guests couldn't have asked for more. All had a leisurely lunch by the water's edge, refreshed themselves in the pool, chatted about things to come and simply enjoyed the day. It was getting on, so Jack, Mildred, Peep and the chauffeur of course packed it in to continue their journey.

It was time to head back to the main house, for they had gone quite a distance and dusk would be setting in by the time they returned. So, off they went. Our crew thanked Hoppy and his entourage for the tour. One must be gracious to a host. You never know when you're going to need them, and you wouldn't want to get on the bad side of a giant hare, especially if you happen to live there. Not a good idea! The drive back was pleasant, but a little quiet. It had been a very interesting day so far, but all were a bit exhausted, with the heat not helping things either.

On arriving back at the mansion, Jack and Mildred headed to the cottage for a short rest before dinner. The couple then dressed for the occasion and proceeded to the main house. Mary had outdone herself once again. A five star restaurant could not have put on a better spread. I have come to the conclusion that Mary Poppins must have gone to the Cordon Blue Culinary School, but never told anyone. I have no idea why she would want to keep this a secret but to each his own. After supper, cocktails were served and later everyone retired for the evening.

The following day, a visit to another section of the ranch was scheduled. Everyone piled into the landrover and our crew left for the unknown. We will call this the unknown because no one had been in this section for some time and that sounds like a good enough reason to me. The direction they headed in took our travelers to the red kangaroo zone. These kangaroos were much larger than your normal ones. And not all of them were red. Some were a little on the pinkish side with some having polka dots. But here they went with the majority vote, and that would be red. These marsupials had an image to maintain and a bit of a macho attitude. It was quite the spectacle to behold. Even Peep hadn't known about the polka dot ones. I wish I had been there when she saw these things hopping all over the place. Wouldn't that be a sight to see! Well, on with our story. Gilbert, the main man here, or should I say kangaroo, met them at the entrance. He was very courteous and pleasant to the guests. He explained the operations of the colony here and of course the reasons for the polka dot kangaroos. You see, there had been, long ago, one special kangaroo with a bit of a genetic problem. This factor had resulted in the appearance of the polka dots on a few of their species. Other than their pigmentation, there was nothing physically wrong with them. No one really knew about them, Gilbert wanted to keep this news as quiet as possible. If you had polka dots in your family, wouldn't you want to keep it quiet? I really hope, for your sake, that you don't have to think about this question very long. Anyway, on with the show.

After a lengthy visit, Jack, Mildred and Peep were on their way. They headed back to Mutton 123 to finish off the day with a relaxing barbecue by the pool. Things went well that night. It wasn't till the next morning when the trouble started. I told you something was coming!

Digit arrived at the house early the next morning with distressing news. Sheep 1-10 were missing. Acronis had double-checked his count and it had turned out to be accurate. Maybe the counting sheep 1-10 had just wandered off and would return later in the day. Everyone would just have to wait and see. By nightfall they were still missing. Peep started to get worried. Her sheep had never done anything like this before. This was so unlike them. Counting sheep are usually a very loyal bunch. That is one of their traits. This was another reason they were so valuable and rare. Little Bo Peep had the only counting sheep farm in her world. They were only native to here and nowhere else. The following morning the news was even worse. Sheep 11-20 were missing. This was becoming quite annoying to Peep. Even Acronis could not locate them. They seemed to have disappeared into thin air. Surely, there had to be an explanation. Every night, more counting sheep were vanishing, ten at a time. This was beginning to get irritating in more ways than one! The repercussions were starting to take effect.

You see, the counting sheep were scheduled for commercials in one week. All the details had been taken care of – the camera crew, the producers, the directors, and the filmmakers. Airline tickets had been booked well in advance for the sheep. To reschedule would be very costly. This was just not acceptable. Something had to be done and quickly at that. Peep had no choice but to call in the International Chicken Rangers. The Rangers arrived the next day. They had chartered a jet in order to expedite the matter. Serta wanted answers and were not willing to wait! Too much was at stake.

So the Chicken Rangers set up their surveillance and waited. The first night there, they could hear a strange sound coming from the fields. At first they weren't sure, then realized it was a ghostly flute sound. Every night, it was the same thing. They knew they had heard this sound before, but could not put their finger on it. After some research, our heroes discovered that it was the same tune played in the fairy tale of the Pied Piper. Now, this was really getting baffling. Pied Piper was a good guy. Why would he be stealing the counting sheep? They set up a trap and hoped it would work. On the remaining sheep, they installed radio frequency tracking devices. They had the technology you know. Then, that night, just after the music started, the rangers followed the sheep. Our four legged friends headed towards the canyon. Once there, they entered one of the deep caverns that led underground. The trap worked and finally the culprit was apprehended. As it turned out, it was Pied Piper. When his original flute had broken, he had gone to the wizard and purchased a replacement. To no ones knowledge, the flute had been cursed by the evil sheep demon Aesop the Second. He was the son of Aesop the First. Aesop had turned against the counting sheep when his credit rating went bad and Serta refused his order. So, he plotted to destroy the Serta Posturepedic Company by depriving them of all their counting sheep. A spell had been put on Pied Piper so that he would not question their orders. To Aesop's dismay, the Chicken Rangers had arrived and saved the day! Now that all the counting sheep were located, something had to be done about Pied Piper. The spell must be broken and Pied returned to his fairy tale. For this, a specialist must be called in. And of course it could be none other than Madame Tousseau. She was the best in her field. Pied was brought to Mutton 123 and kept under strict supervision till she could arrive. An urgent e-mail was sent requesting her presence, informing her that this was of the utmost importance. Madame Tousseau caught the red-eye that night , arriving the next morning. She realized the gravity of the situation and was ready to give it her all.

A special room was prepared for Pied's decantation. He was brought in and sat down opposite the psychic. She had brought her Book of Shadows just in case. She had no knowledge of how strong Aesop's powers were. She had performed this ceremony before, but not with regards to counting sheep. But not to worry, the Book of Shadows would see her through. It had never failed her in the past. Madame Tousseau opened the famous book and hit the jackpot! The exact spell she needed lay directly in front of her. On reciting the incantation, a fog enveloped the room and an eerie sound began. The crystal ball in front of her opened and the demons were drawn into it. If you've ever seen Jumangi, you'd know what I mean. Pied went limp, almost falling over and then sat upright. A spirit seem to leave him at the same time the crystal ball opened. It was the evil spirits removing themselves from his body. When all was over, Pied Piper looked around with a bewildered mind. Madame Tousseau explained to him what had happened. She promised to return him to his fairy tale promptly. Turning the pages in her precious book, she instructed him to sit very still and not be afraid. He did so. After the second spell, Pied was no longer. He had been successfully returned to his place in history. Madame Tousseau collected her fee, packed her belongings and was on her way for she had a busy schedule that week elsewhere. Everyone was elated to know the mystery of the missing counting sheep was over. I forgot to mention that Aesop the Second never returned to Mutton 123 again. Before leaving, Madame Tousseau had cast a protective spell over the sheep and Aesop was never seen again, not even to this day.

Everything was back in order at Mutton 123. Peep was happy; the counting sheep were back where they belonged, and the Serta Posturepedic Co. was back in business. All in all, things turned out pretty good. And just in time too. The sheep could meet their deadline next week.

That night, all our characters slept peacefully – no more stress, no more worries! Jack and Mildred could leave knowing everything was right with Little Bo Peep and her counting sheep. Before they left our couple took a day to drive up the coast for a leisurely afternoon by themselves. Turning off the main road, they discovered the most beautiful cove they had ever seen - so peaceful, so serene, so sheltered. In this cove, a sailboat was anchored. They could see people on board and waved. To their surprise, it was Puff. Remember Puff, the magic dragon? In his fairy tale, he had lost Jackie Paper. It seems Jackie had not left forever. He had gone to visit his mother who had not been feeling quite herself. The fairy tale had ended before his return, so this is why no one knew he and Puff were reunited. Jackie and Puff had been sailing the coast while on an extended leave of absence from their story. As it turned out, they were headed to Fairy Island. Puff had some unfinished business to attend to before he and Jackie returned to their tale. Since the Fire Breather- that's what they called their boat – had the same destination as Jack and Mildred, the couple were invited to join Puff and Jackie on their trip. Now, I ask you, who could beat a deal like that? This was definitely an offer that couldn't be refused! The two adventurers accepted their host's gracious offer, but would have to return to Mutton 123 to collect their belongings and say goodbye to Peep and all who resided there. Arrangements were made to depart the next morning. Jack and Mildred journeyed back to the ranch and spent the rest of the day with Peep. It would be a long time before Jack would see Peep again, so the two wanted to spend the remainder of the day together. That evening, everyone sat down to one of Mary's delicious meals. Drinks were served on the patio then all retired for the night. Jack and Mildred had to meet Puff and Jackie quite early and the two wanted to be alert and refreshed for their journey.

The next morning, bright and early, Jack and Mildred arrived at the peer where Puff and Jackie were anchored. It was a beautiful day with blue skies and sunshine. Sailing should be relaxing for the seas were calm and serene. After everyone was aboard the Fire Breather, they set off on their journey. It was approximately a four-day cruise to Fairy Island. Jackie had checked with the weather channel so as not to encounter any storms along the way. This had turned out to be a better vacation than anticipated for Jack and Mildred. This sailing thing would be a real blast!

It turned out that Puff and Jackie had quite the set up on the vessel. The guests were escorted to their sleeping quarters and told to come up on deck when ready. The bar would be open and it was time to relax. A celebration was in order and these guys knew how to celebrate! The Pina Coladas kept coming and the Electric Popsicles went down like lemonade. This would definitely quench anyone's thirst. Maybe a little too much! Or so it seemed by the looks of them at this point in time. It wasn't long with the heat, the sun, and the drinks before everyone lay on deck fast asleep. I know one should not drink and drive, but Puff had no worries since he had set the correct course and put the Fire Breather on autopilot. The anchor system was fully automated and set to drop at 7:00 p.m. that evening. You can see why they need not worry. Don't you wish you had a set up like that on your boat? Imagine the partying you could do then! Maybe we best leave that alone. It could get a little scary.

It was about 10:00 p.m. when life started to return on the Fire Breather. After taking their Advil, or Tylenol, whichever works – we don't want to be biased here – everyone crawled into his or her respective beds – this is a clean story – to sleep off the rest of the festivities. They would start fresh the next morning. And that they did, vowing never to do this again. I'll bet you've said those words before! With one day gone and three to go, all decided that the rest of the trip should be a sober one. An occasional drink would be acceptable, but no more partying, not like the night before. That day everything went smoothly with no mishaps. The weather channel had been true to its word. Now, there's fiction if I ever heard it! Only in a fairy tale of course!

We will now leave our sailors and delve into another realm of fantasy for a short time. Don't worry, it will all fall into place when I'm done. Hasn't it always in the past?

Long ago, once upon a time - there's a cliché if I ever heard one – lived a little mermaid named Miranda. She was a petite little thing with long silky blonde hair; skin of arabesque, and royal blue scales soft and supple. If I recall correctly, the last time I was talking to her, she mentioned that Skin So Smooth was her cream of choice. I purchased some after that, and let me tell you, it really does do wonders. No need for "The

Swan" after using this stuff! Anyway, that's not what
I'm here to tell you. Shall we go on? Miranda lived in
the Enchanted Garden beneath the sea. It was a magical place where humming fish flit among the flowers
of the coral reef. They would sip the sweet nectar of
the velvety petals and opalescent hues that called to
them. Amidst the splendor of luxuriant blossoms the
humming fish would ride on crystalline whirls of the
magnificent gardenscape of Miranda's domain. Here,
mermaids roamed wherever they wished without any
threat from the outside world. Even pirates weren't
allowed here, especially Blackbeard. Did you know he
had a thing for mermaids? They did, and that is why
you will never see Blackbeard sail these waters. Miranda
could not have asked for a better world. The one thing
that was missing in her life was her true love, Charlie.
Now Charlie was a little different. He was a tuna. But
Miranda, being who she was, loved Charlie with all her
heart and soul. Everyday, she would swim along the
waters surrounding the Enchanted Garden and look for
him. Charlie had left long ago in order to pursue his
dream of becoming an actor. He had vowed to Miranda
that he would return for her one day and that she never
forget him. This she did, for Miranda was true blue (in
more ways than one). She truly believed that Charlie
would return and the two would live happily ever after
in the Enchanted Garden. As you know, Charlie did
make it to the big screen. I'm sure you've seen his commercials. But, unfortunately, it didn't last as long as he

would have liked. Being cast in bit parts here and there was not the life Charlie had expected. You see, when the sponsors had cancelled his contract, due to lack of interest in the tuna business, our forlorn friend had to find other work. As you know, there isn't a lot out there for an aging tuna. So, bit parts became a temporary way of life. Now, remember, I said temporary. Charlie was not happy with this life, so he made a decision to change it. He would go back to the sea and reunite with his beloved. Now, Charlie wasn't too bad off. He had made some good investments over time and had quite the nest egg built up. Enough for him and Miranda to have a good life together without worries. Actually, it doesn't take much to live on when you're a creature of the sea. You don't have to pay taxes, heating bills; insurance, and housing costs are at a minimum. You never have to stand in line at the grocery store, and g.s.t. doesn't exist. What better world could there be!

So Charlie went on his way, heading for the ocean. The Enchanted Garden was located in the Pacific. We cannot divulge the exact location, for that would be totally unethical. And we just don't do that here! It was a long journey but Charlie knew Miranda was worth it. He would swim and swim, then rest for a while. This process would continue till he reached his destination. He knew it would take about a week. He had prepared for the long trip with great care. Luggage was kept to a minimum. Anything else he had acquired while away was put in storage till further notice. The weather stayed clear so Charlie had smooth sailing all the way through. Nourishment for the trip would be picked up along the way. A tuna could do this, you know. And Charlie had this part down to a science. How do you think he had survived to such a ripe old age? He had a lot of zip for a senior tuna, especially when it came to Miranda. Amazing what viagra will do for you! It sure kept Charlie young – not a gray scale in sight. Enough of this, let's go on.

When Charlie finally arrived at the Enchanted Garden, Miranda was there waiting for him. She was absolutely elated to see him. She had known his e.t.a. for he had called her. I told you Zucchini Telecom was everywhere. You didn't believe me, did you? Now, you know. The two embraced, held fins, and looked into each other's eyes knowing that Charlie was ready to settle down. You had to be there. It was quite the reunion! Now that Charlie is back, we have to do something about this species thing. Miranda being a mermaid and Charlie being a tuna just won't work unless we fix it. And so we shall. As in all the other problems in this story, a specialist was called in. Now this is a little different than the other times. We're talking species here. That's a tall order to fill, but we have just the expert. Word spread through the grapevine, and fell upon the ears of the most famous wizard of them all – Merlin. This one was a new one for him and Merlin thought he would like to give it a shot. As usual, an e-mail was sent to the Enchanted Garden notifying the residents there of his time of arrival. Much had to be done to prepare for his appearance. The gardens were cleared of any weeds. The flowers were fluffed, petals spayed for any defects, and arranged with meticulous care. Things must be perfect, for it is not everyday that a famous visitor like Merlin bestows his presence upon one's domain. Miranda and Charlie oversaw the preparations. Nothing must be overlooked. And nothing was. The Enchanted Garden looked magnificent when all was finished.

Merlin arrived with all the splendor this underwater world could muster. And believe me, they knew how to muster! His presence was announced throughout the H20 kingdom. It's not everyday that such a great wizard displays his presence. Very few beings of any kind have actually seen Merlin. They have only heard of him. I'm hear to tell you he is real and not just a myth in people's minds. Enough of this, let's get on with our adventure. Merlin met with Miranda and Charlie to study the situation and devise a plan. Opening his "Magic Book of Spells ", which he had brought with him, just in case, for it had been a while. Unknown to most, Merlin had taken his retirement early and had not practiced magic in a bit. He didn't want to blow this. The repercussions would be disastrous should he mess this up. So, he double-checked his book just to be sure. It was there all right in big bold red letters. When the scene was set for the change and all items required were in place, Merlin sat Miranda and Charlie down in front of him. They were to be very still and quiet. Merlin stared at them with an intense look on his face. His eyes seemed to look right through them. On the count of three, he cast the magic spell. The waters surrounding them turned a dark murky aqua colour. What seemed like hours was only seconds. When all was said and done, Charlie was no longer a tuna. He was now a male sea nymph. Merlin had decided that life would be a lot longer for them both if he turned Charlie into a male mermaid (sea nymph) rather than Miranda into a tuna. Besides, have you ever heard of canned mermaid? But you have heard of canned tuna. Between you and I, I think Merlin made the right choice. And this is why to this day; Charlie the tuna is no longer heard of.

Miranda and Charlie were so happy; they invited Merlin to the wedding. They had waited too long already. The happy event was planned to take place in a couple of days. Merlin could not stay much longer than that. Since Miranda had always planned to marry Charlie, she already had her trousseau. So that task was out of the way. Since no time was available for sending out invitations, word was passed on through the locals and it didn't take long before everyone knew of the festive event. Arrangements were made to have the president of the "Sea Creatures Association "preside over the ceremony and Merlin to bless the marriage. Both were glad to oblige. The flowers of the Enchanted Garden came out in full force to line the aisle and the finest of the sea chairs were set up. The reception would take place in the great hall of the garden. As you would expect, a seafood buffet was put out with great care by the finest chefs of the realm. When all was in place, the ceremony began. It was the event of the sea world. Everyone who was anyone was in attendance. Miranda and Charlie could not have asked for a more beautiful wedding. They would remember this auspicious occasion for the rest of their days.

Now, if you recall, earlier in our story, Jack, Mildred, Puff and Jackie were sailing to the thriving metropolis of Fairy Island. Weather had been good, so they had no worries, so far. Somewhere along the way, the Fire Breather had gone off course without them realizing it. The auto system that Puff had installed picked up a virus somehow and this threw them off. Our crew of adventurers weren't quite sure where they were at this point in time. This is where Miranda and Charlie come in. The two honeymooners had been swimming near the point where the Fire Breather had ended up. The sailing vessel had anchored for the night when Charlie spotted them. He thought this unusual for very few boats ever came here. In fact, this was only the second one that had been located in the area for quite some time. Being evening, Miranda and Charlie would wait till morning to check it out.

The very next morning, our crew awakened to find the Pisces pair lurking around the vessel. When asked what they were doing there, Miranda and Charlie explained to them the situation that had brought them here. In exchange, Puff informed them of their dilemma. The problem was solved when Miranda and Charlie said they would guide them to their destination for our swimmers were headed in that direction anyway. With all problems put to rest, our characters were on their way. So, the Fire Breather, Puff, Jackie, Mildred, Jack, Miranda and Charlie headed for Fairy Island. I told you it all fit. I'll bet you weren't quite so sure this time, were you? Never doubt the writer. I know the story better than you do. After all, I wrote it.

Late the following evening, the Fire Breather sailed into port at Fairy Island. They tied up for the night and would take care of business later. A good night's sleep would do them all good. Everyone awoke the next morning to a bright sunny day. There on the peer stood Molaki with his sidekick Sebastian. This arrival they had not anticipated. Since the technical problems on the Fire Breather, Puff and Jackie had not been able to access the Internet, so Fiona could not be notified of their e.t.a. Molaki recognized the Fire Breather, since Puff had been there before. But he did not know of Jack and Mildred's presence on the vessel. Once aware of them, he called Queen Fiona immediately. As always she was quick to send the carriage for them. The three blind mice were called in, as they were on standby, and the carriage made ready for Fiona's visitors. Remember Cinderella's buggy, well this is the same one. Jack and Mildred said their goodbyes to Puff and Jackie thanking them for the lift to their destination. Puff and Jackie were given an open invitation to Southfork should the two ever venture to that part of the world. Wouldn't that be a sight to see! Puff the magic dragon and Jackie Paper checking out Dallas. You never know, they may enjoy going to Gilley's. One never knows about these things. On with our story.

The carriage arrived in all its grandeur. What other way would you expect a Queen to do it? Protocol must be maintained no matter what. After all, she is the Queen of Fairy Island. The carriage took them on a quick tour of the area, then on to King Albert and Queen Fiona's residence. The triads were quite gracious to our guests for Fiona had informed them of their arrival. It had been a long time since they had seen each other, but Fiona greeted Mildred with open arms. Jack and Albert retired to the drawing room to get to know one another while Fiona and Mildred strolled through the gardens reminiscing old times and bringing Fiona up to date concerning the outside world. Later on, cocktails were served on the upper patio - they had a lower one too - and all enjoyed the evening. Jack and Mildred were shown to their quarters where they retired for the night. Mildred was so happy to see her long lost cousin; she could not believe her good fortune. She was in such a good mood, we won't tell you what happened next. Use your imagination. Let's just say, Jack woke up the next day with a big smile on his face! Need I say more? If I have to, you have some major issues to deal with, and that's no joke!

The next day a luncheon was planned to introduce Jack and Mildred to the rest of Fiona and Albert's entourage. Molaki and Sebastian were there along with O'Reilly and a few of Fiona and Albert's closest friends. Fiona pulled out all the stops on this one. Even magic graced the table. In the center stood a large pedestal bowl with the oddest beans anyone outside of Fairy Land had ever seen. These happened to be the famous jumping beans. The beans were quite excited for they had not been brought out in quite a while. Fiona had to inform them of proper etiquette when out in public. They agreed and finally settled down. All in all everyone had a great time and so friendly too. Jack and Mildred were quite impressed with the residents here. It was all Toronado and Daisy said it was and more. No wonder they had such a great time when they were here. After the festivities were over Fiona took Mildred aside for a private conversation. Mildred seemed baffled for Fiona 's tone turned to serious. If you thought things were a little weird before, just wait!

Fiona told Mildred that the realm of magic had been waiting for her for a very long time. This statement put Mildred's curiosity in high gear. A family secret had been buried long ago when their great great grandmother had left this world. She had been the Great Empress in the World of the Unreal. She had left what was called in fairyland a "letter of destiny" that was to be opened only when her rightful heir came to be. Mildred still could not fathom what this had to do with her. She's about to find out and it's a whopper! Fiona explained to her that she, Mildred, was the heir that all waited for. Mildred was astonished at the news. An inheritance of great importance had been waiting for her. The letter stated that the heir would make herself present and all would know. This scripture was the key to a realm that had been sealed for thousands of years. You have to remember, in the world of magic, time is not of the essence. What are years to us are seconds to them. I know this for a fact because I've been there and back. At least that's what people have told me. Regardless, Fiona's time was now. The royal scripture had stated as much. Destiny must be fulfilled. Fiona brought Mildred through a long tunnel under the castle where, in front of them, stood a doorway, with golden triads, in statue form of course, on either side of it. The triads were of the finest gold crystalline that ever was. They had to be statues. No one could stay on their feet that long! Embossed on the great doors was the Royal Seal. The seal, written in fairy hieroglyphics, represented a world that had been hidden in time since the Great Empress's demise. It was written that Mildred should take her rightful place here once the seal was broken. All those who had tried in the past, with no avail of course, to break the seal had perished. Only the true heir to the realm would be successful. Fiona knew in her heart that Mildred was the one. Mildred nervously took the golden saber that lay to the side and opened the seal. The great doors opened to reveal a kingdom beyond even imagination. Even you won't be able to guess this one!

This was the realm of the "Great Creator". A world where magic began and ended. A place where reality had no existence and time just a myth.

One part of this world involved all the fairy tales that ever were and would ever be. It worked this way. On one side stood a time clock and on the other side the entry and exit. When a fairy tale was requested by the outside world, a requisition form was filled out and sent through the proper channels. From there a priority message was forwarded to the requested characters for the tale. At this point in the process, the players would go to the checkout point, collect the props for the story and proceed to uploads, punch the time clock and be transferred to their proper destination. This way all areas were covered so as to prevent confusion when a tale was requested. Also this ensured accurate records for the overseer of the realm of the "Great Creator". When a fairy tale ended, the characters would return here and log in. This method kept things running smoothly. Our government should take a lesson from these guys!

Another part of the realm –the one that had been sealed from the rest of the world for thousands of years – held all the mythical creatures of time. Here lived the dragons, the beings of astrology, creatures of the Greek mythology, and we mustn't forget the famous creatures of Jurassic Park. Where do you think they came from? Now you know the truth according to this writer anyway. To unleash this part of the realm on reality would be disastrous. If you've seen "Jurassic Park" you know what I mean! This was an extremely important aspect of the overseer's occupation. You see, there existed a protective force field that kept the world of imagination safe from the evil that dwelled here. I told you this was going to get a little weird didn't I? Now, do you believe me? I wouldn't lie to you, honest!

Long long ago, this had been a place of peaceful existence. Then one day, for a reason that has yet to be revealed, evil had taken hold and life as it was changed. Creatures normally courteous and gentle had turned on each other and the rest of their world. Survival of the fittest had become the motto to live by. This was so unlike the life that had been here before. So, in order to protect the domain of imagination, a force field was put in place so the evil that existed here could not spread and destroy all the good in the fairy tale realm. Until this evil issue could be solved, all residents of this community would be kept under this so-called house arrest. Now this is where Mildred comes into the picture. Being the true heir of the realm of the Great Creator, only she who was destined to rule could put history back into place. And let me tell you, that's one tall order to fill! You couldn't give me this job under any circumstances! Does this remind you of something? If you haven't guessed it yet, it is the world of politics. Do you see the resemblance? If you haven't, obviously you don't listen to the news. And I won't take that any farther.

Now, we left Fiona and Mildred back in the great chamber if you recall. When all was said and done, Mildred had some major brainstorming to do on this one. She wasn't sure whether she could fill these shoes or that she even wanted to. Her life back at Southfork was a good one. Mildred wasn't ready to give up life, as she knew it with Jack. And what of the children? Could they cope with this existence? I think not! So, after many hours of deliberation, and of course consulting with Jack, because he is after all a part of this, whether he liked it or not, Mildred had come to the conclusion that a way out had to be found. She would discuss it with Fiona in the morning. Definitely a must! This job didn't come with an instruction manual. So, the next best thing to do would be to go to the expert for advice. And this would be Fiona.

After a hearty breakfast at the local fairy club diner, Fiona and Mildred had a heart to heart concerning the situation. As in anything else, there is always a loophole if one searches hard enough. And between the two of them, they found it. Fiona would look in the Book of Magic Scriptures for the answer that would benefit all parties. Mildred and Fiona proceeded to the secret room where the famous book was kept. Before they could do this task, Fiona had to reveal to Mildred certain issues regarding the "Book". Now, this was a magical book. On laying eyes upon it, one must be true to heart or it would not speak. Mildred, being the person she was, knew this would not be a problem. On arriving at the location intended, Fiona carefully pulled the book from the shelf, now held in the famous Archive of Magic, and placed it on the table. On the cover of the book was a pair of eyes that looked deep in her soul. The eyes seemed at peace. This was a good sign Fiona told Mildred. The book opened itself, and then greeted Mildred. It was as if it understood. The pages turned and there in front of them were the answers they were searching for. In a special ceremony, Mildred could turn the power she inherited over to Fiona. The book then informed the two of the details of this ritual and the precision that must be maintained throughout. In order that nothing be left to chance, Book sent the details to the printer in order that they would each have a copy. After the ceremony, the copies were to be destroyed by fire, not a paper shredder! This, Book was emphatic on. Fiona and Mildred were elated. They would do exactly as Book instructed, to the letter! Consequences would be disastrous should they screw up. And you know how that feels, don't you? We've all been there at least once!

Next day, preparations were commenced for the sacred ceremony. This process would take place in the great ritual room. Here, centrally located in the center of the room – on a platform (that wasn't made of plywood either)- stood a gigantic altar. Book was to be placed here, as requested. On each side of Book was a pair of ornate candles on magnificent golden holders.

These were not of the ordinary. They had been passed down through time and generations from the table of King Arthur of Camelot. Located strategically in front of the altar was an eight by eight area with crystal flooring. Under this area could be seen a pool of pale blue translucent water that sparkled when gazed upon. Book had been very specific concerning the details. So every step in this process was followed to the letter. Special lighting had to be ordered in for the occasion. So, an urgent order was placed with e-bay for the necessities. This was the quickest way. The next day the important package arrived. Good thing they didn't order through Canada Post –they'd still be waiting! And can you imagine if the order had been lost! Have you ever had to track something lost in the mail? Can you imagine! Mildred would be in a senior citizens home by then! Enough of the wise cracks. Back to our story. After all was in place, Mildred had to be made ready for the occasion. The sacred garments that had been in storage were taken out, sent to the Quick Cleaners of Fairy Land, and returned promptly. Fiona, being a local, already had the proper apparel. One more item on the agenda and they would be ready. The major players had to be brought in and these were biggies! E-mail was sent to King Arthur and Queen Genevieve of Camelot requiring them to preside over the ceremony. In her e-mail, Fiona informed them of Book's insistence that only they perform such a task. It was of the utmost importance. An answer came almost immediately. You see, Genevieve had been at her computer when the request had come in. Since she had high speed, time was not a problem. No dial up here! The royal pair would leave the next morning for Fairy Land. King Arthur and Queen Genevieve had no need for instructions as they had performed this type of ceremony in the past. They knew the routine. The next evening, our visitors arrived as scheduled. Chicken Wings Express had pulled out all the stops on this one. It's not everyday that you get passengers of this caliber! The airline felt extremely honored to be the royal carriers of such auspicious beings of the realm of imagination.

The following afternoon, at approximately 2:00 p.m. our time, the ceremony began. Mildred was brought in and told to stand on the crystal floor in front of the great altar. Fiona was to stand to her right, just off the designated area. King Arthur and Queen Genevieve stood at the altar facing Mildred. Between them and Mildred was the famous stone. Embedded in this stone – or boulder, whichever you want to call it – was the Jeweled Sword. It was a sight to behold, laden with emeralds, rubies, and diamonds. Only the elite of the fairy world were allowed attendance. After all, this was a secret ceremony. Together King Arthur and Queen Genevieve recited the required incantation. Then, Arthur proceeded to the stone. Here, he took hold of the Sword and pulled it from the stone. Then, he walked over to Mildred and touched each of her shoulders with the Sword. He spoke words of unknown language, and then nodded to Fiona to come and place herself beside Mildred. Arthur then repeated the process with Fiona. Afterwards, Arthur walked over to the stone. His eyes gazed upon it as if in a trance. He held the Sword high with both hands and brought it down slowly till it touched the stone. Upon saying words taken from the Book of Magic Scriptures, Arthur pushed the Sword back into the stone. Almost at once, a great blinding light filled the room and a mystical haze smothered the air. As the great light dulled and the haze lifted Mildred and Fiona bowed their heads and recited the sacred oath that had been written centuries ago by the mighty Orb. Just so you know, in case I haven't mentioned it, the mighty Orb was the literary genius of the realm of imagination. It was his job to write all things sacred and honorable in his world. And he was the very best; for he had received the Pulitzer Prize for Literature ten years running in Fairy Land. After the dust settled, the ceremony was complete. Fiona was now officially the new heir to the realm of the Great Creator.

Now Mildred and Jack could return to Southfork knowing all was well with her cousin and that history would be put right. It had been quite the adventure for our travelers. Definitely not boring, that's for sure! But it was now time to get back home. Even with all this excitement Jack and Mildred missed the children one through twelve inclusive and the remainder of their family at Southfork. They informed Fiona that the pair would be leaving as soon as reservations could be made with Chicken Wings Express. Fiona and Albert understood. So, Fiona, being the gracious and caring person she was, would look after this ASAP. It would be a lot easier if she handled things. When she spoke, the airlines listened! It didn't take long to make the arrangements. Mildred and Jack would depart in two days. This would give the couple time to relax. With everything that had happened, a little quiet time with their cousin had been a rarity. A barbecue was planned for that evening. Even Fairy Land knew about barbecues. Of course, they usually stay a little more sober than we do. They do not consider Pina Coladas a necessity for such an event. And we'll leave it at that!

Two days later it was time to depart. Jack and Mildred said their goodbyes to all and boarded Chicken Wings Express. They would be home soon. Both were looking forward to seeing everyone at Southfork. As the saying goes, it's nice to get away, but always feels good to be home again. After all, home is where the heart is and their hearts belonged to Dallas.

Jack and Mildred arrived safely. The flight had been a pleasant one. Fiona had arranged for them to fly first class. Chicken Wings Express had outdone themselves. Not just because of the fact that if they screwed up, Fiona and Albert were the ones to answer to, but this airline was one that held passenger treatment to the highest standard. Try and find an airline like that now without it costing your life savings! Good luck!

All were present to meet them at Dallas International. The children were elated to see them. Bernard and Ophillia had taken good care of the children but it wasn't the same as mom and dad. It never is. All in all, things had run pretty smooth while Jack and Mildred had been away. A welcome back supper was planned with all the trimmings. Later, Jack and Mildred would sit with the family and tell of their fantastic voyage. All ears would be on them for sure, especially the children one through twelve inclusive. One of these days we'll give them names but for now this is the way it has to be.

We will leave our characters now in peace till our next adventure and see you in chapter 5. You never know what's coming so use your imagination. See if yours is as good as this author's.

CHAPTER 5

Well, guess what, we're back. The crew at Southfork missed you so much they had to return and see how you're doing. Now I know it's been a little strange up to now, but not to worry it gets better. What else would you expect from this unorthodox author?

Now if you remember from chapter 4 all were back at Southfork resting up from their adventures or misadventures. It all depends on how you look at it. We won't even try to analyze that one. I'll leave that up to you.

Daisy had gone and picked up the morning mail. It was a beautiful sunny day and she was still working on her profile. Every morning she would walk to get the latest news from the mailbox. This was her morning exercise, which is more than most of us do. It just happened that amongst the junk mail was a flyer. Now this flyer advertised a summer camp for children. According to the information supplied in this so-called junk mail a new modern summer camp had recently opened up. According to the info, an open house was being held this weekend coming in order that potential clients could preview the facility. This sounded quite interesting. The children One through Twelve inclusive had been asking about camp lately. School would be out in just a few weeks and as you know, if you've ever had them, children can get a little excited when it comes to vacation time. This was definitely worth checking out. So, Daisy informed Jack and Mildred of this, showed them the flyer, and it was decided that this should be put on their to do list for the weekend. They would inform the children when they returned from school.

Now, I know we called them One through Twelve inclusive throughout the story, but I really do think it time to give them actual names. So, to keep it simple we will call them the following: One, Two, Three, Four, Five, Six, Seven, Eight, Nine, Ten, Eleven, Twelve. I don't know about you, but this seems logical and easy to remember, especially if your memory isn't quite what it used to be. I do hope this simplifies things for you. Now, if you happen to be numerically challenged, you're in trouble and I can't help you there. Now that that is settled, let's go on.

It was decided that the entire family living at South-fork would go on Saturday and have a look at this children's entertainment center. When One, Two, Three, Four, Five, Six, Seven, Eight, Nine, Ten, Eleven, Twelve arrived home from school, Jack and Mildred told them of their plans. The children were ecstatic. When you were a kid, and your parents told you that you might be going to camp I'll bet you were happy too. Just imagine, three weeks with no parents! We know this is every kid's dream holiday!

Well, Saturday came and all members of the household were up bright and early to prepare for the outing. After the children finished bouncing off the walls, a hearty breakfast was had by all and preparations made for the day's sightseeing tour. The facility was located approximately 100 miles from Southfork. Far enough but not too far thought Jack and Mildred. With the children as excited as they were, all adults put on their earplugs to avoid you know what! I shouldn't have to tell you that one. This way, all would arrive in a pleasant mood, not pulling their hair, or feathers out!

All in all it worked out well and our crew arrived at the facility with time to spare. After taking a quick survey of the place, Jack and Mildred decided it was quite the spread. This just may work out after all. Even the children One through Twelve inclusive were impressed and that took some doing.

I will now give you some info on the place. At one time in history, to no one's knowledge, not even the historians, this castle belonged to none other than Dracula's cousin, through marriage of course, Gilbert Darkenbaum. He had immigrated to North America in order to avoid persecution in his homeland. Even though he himself was not an evil person, his association with Dracula was enough to cause concern to the locals. So, rather than go through all the hassles necessary, Gilbert thought it best if he just left. And that he did. We're not sure how he got here, but we definitely know he made it and successfully at that.

The castle was surrounded by a wide moat and protected by a concrete wall 12 feet high. Something like Fort Knox but a whole lot more fun. The enclosure encompassed fifty acres of prime land, with beautiful meadows, streams of crystal clear water filled with brook trout (for those who enjoyed the art of fishing) magnificent forests (not too large of course) and wonderful aromatic gardens everywhere. Now I know children don't always appreciate this kind of thing, so in order to make it appealing to the younger generation, a tennis court, swimming pool, hot tub area, and other such things were included. There was nothing left to chance here. After all, this was a class A camp. It had even made it into the "World Book of Better Camps ". But, as always, there was something a little strange about the place. Gilbert was a bit of an eccentric on certain subjects. One of his phobias was evil spirits. He really didn't want them hanging out here. So, he did what any normal eccentric would do. He had giant stone garlic buds set on the great wall every 500 yards. Gilbert figured with enough of them, the evil spirits that haunted his past would not grace his table with their presence. By the way, this also included were-wolves, just so you know.

Tall poplars lined the drive up to the main house. The entrance seemed to rise out of nowhere. An immense stairway, not too high though, led up to the ornately carved doors that signaled the main entrance to the residence. One knew that these doors belonged here for they had been embedded with large crystal garlic buds. Gilbert was taking no chances whatsoever. Just in case a spirit managed to slip through the main gates, they would not get into the house. As you can see, Gilbert was somewhat of a fanatic when it came to superstition, especially after the fiasco in his homeland. But then you already knew that of course. Let's face it, anyone who wants that much garlic around must be a bit on the odd side, don't you agree? Now after all this, one would expect to see gray stonewalls with dark floors and somewhat of a somber décor. Just the opposite here. Floors were of the best oak one could acquire and shine like you would not believe. You could see your reflection as if in a mirror. Walls were of a light crème color giving the whole scene a warm and inviting ambiance. Large windows allowed sunlight to fill the rooms no matter where you went in the place. Ceilings were beamed intermittently with rich mahogany wood giving the structure an air of grandeur. Each room had a set of large French doors that opened onto spectacular gardens. This seemed more like a luxury resort than a refurbished castle. All in all, it was quite the spectacle.

Flowers from the gardens filled the rooms with the sweet scent of magnolias, roses, lilies, and all the aromatic flowers that one could imagine. The décor inside was bright with a mixture of old and new, but done with exquisite taste (not like some of the decorating disasters we've all seen at one time or another).

On arriving, a guide greeted our crew at the door, giving them a bit of info on the history of the place while guiding them through the many facets of the castle. Adjacent to the foyer was a large great room, as they are called nowadays. Off the great room was an immense dining hall with a capacity for seating 100. A long walnut table surrounded by comfortable and lavish chairs adorned the center of the room. Magnificent works of art from ancient times (we won't mention which times- don't want to scare the children or put off potential clients) hung on the walls in great majesty. Adjacent to the dining hall was a massive kitchen with every modern gadget available. When you're cooking for this many, you need all the help you can get. Off the kitchen area was the staff housing. All employees that worked here resided on the premises with of course, excellent accommodations. The east wing of the castle encompassed the dormitories. Nothing but the best here either. Everything at this facility seemed meticulous and well equipped to handle the needs of all. The surrounding grounds were nothing short of magnificent with tennis courts, archery and soccer fields and such. All sporting activities were made available to the students. Now, you tell me, what child in their right mind wouldn't want to attend a camp like this one. We should have been so lucky when we were kids. All we got were cardboard boxes, old pots and pans, and a sandbox. But we sure managed to have fun anyway. I know I sure did. This was summer camp for the elite it would seem. But not so fast. All children were welcome here. For those without the means government subsidies picked up most of the tab. The rich and the poor- all could attend. This was one of the conditions of Gilbert's will when he passed away or croaked as the term goes. But we won't use that term here. One should have a little more class than that. Now that you have a good description of the place we can continue with our story. Everything seems sweet and innocent so far, doesn't it? Don't worry; it won't stay that way for very long. Do you seriously think I could leave it that way after reading the previous chapters? If you do, we won't talk about your lack of insight. I will say no more on that subject.

Jack and Mildred were so impressed they signed all the children up for camp for 4 weeks. You should have seen the look on the staffs' faces when asked the children's names. They just looked at each other in bewilderment and shook their heads. Nothing could actually be said. These people were their business. So the staff smiled, made nice and kept their thoughts to themselves. Unknown to them, Jack had done his homework and had the place thoroughly checked out.

This way, both could feel at ease about sending the children here. It seems too perfect doesn't it? Just remember, things aren't always, as they seem. You'll find out soon enough. So, it was settled. One through Twelve inclusive would attend camp in one month.

The trip back to Southfork was anything but peaceful. Take 12 kids, show them this, telling them they are going, to a castle to boot, and turn them loose. Now, how quiet do you think that would be? Not my cup of tea, but I'm only writing this story. I don't have to be there. A glutton for punishment I am not! After arriving home, the adults all proceeded to the medicine cabinet for their headache medication and the children sent out to play.

Quick and Quack would not be attending camp at this time. Chicken camp would be the following month. The pair had to wait. But at least they knew they would be going. Also, One through Twelve could give them the heads up on the place when they return. Just what everyone needs - two chickens with an edge!

Four weeks went by fairly quickly with the children getting more agitated on a daily basis. Camp couldn't come soon enough! At least that's what the adults thought. Could you blame them! So, as promised, children One through Twelve inclusive were loaded up with all the necessary equipment required – the camp had given the parents a list of necessities that were a must – and delivered (to the parents relief) to camp. Now I don't know if you noticed or not but I haven't mentioned the name of this camp. Now that you have a picturesque image of it in your mind, I can tell you. It is called Dracula's Haven. You didn't seriously think it would be something normal did you? Wouldn't fit in this story, would it? Maybe at the moment, but not for long!

On arriving at camp, the children said goodbye to Jack and Mildred and ventured inside accompanied by their guide. The children One through Twelve inclusive were led to the East wing where the dormitories were situated. One, Two, Three, Four, Five and Six were situated on one side and Seven, Eight, Nine, Ten, Eleven and Twelve found their rooms directly across the hall. The accommodations were exactly as described in the brochure. It could not have been more perfect.

The children were informed that lunch would be served at 12 noon. Afterwards, an outing through the facility was scheduled in order that they could familiarize themselves with their surroundings. After this was over, the children were told that they would have the rest of the day to wander around and check the place out. And that they did. Now, Twelve was quite curious about the place. He wanted to know more. So, he went to the one area where he presumed he could find this knowledge. Now, if you haven't figured out where this was, you definitely have a minor problem or a very low I.Q. Take your pick. Now, we get to the good part.

In the library was a book. This book held all the history of the castle. It drew Twelve right to it. Twelve was a bit of a bookworm anyway, so this seemed normal to him. His eyes lit up when he opened it. Unknown to him was a map pinpointing all the places of interest. These were not your ordinary interests. On the reverse of this map was a detailed plan of all the secret passages in the castle. Twelve informed all the others of his find. What the children did not know was that this book was off limits to them. They had not read the sign on the shelf. When they did see it, it was too late. So, in order not to get caught, they copied the map - sent it to the printer – (they were computer save`), and would investigate this find at a later date. A vote was held and all agreed to meet here at midnight day after tomor-row. This knowledge would demand the utmost secrecy. After all, they did not want to get caught! No one wants to get into that much trouble. We've all been there a time or two – definitely not fun! In the meantime, Ten, Eleven, and Twelve would study the map. This they did. What I didn't tell you was that Eleven had a photographic memory. Talk about coming in handy. And at just the right time too!

At the precise time planned, all the children met in the library. Eleven knew which wall opened the entrance to the secret passages. He went right to it. And sure enough, it worked. The tunnel it opened onto wasn't very long. It led the children to a room where stone benches lined the walls. In the center stood a round table in which circular carvings were embossed with raised figures of a raven, a cobra, and a sphinx.

These figures seem to glow when the light cast a shadow upon them. A strange aura surrounded them. The children were afraid at first, but when nothing happened, they felt more at ease. Opposite the entrance was a large oval stone as if blocking an entrance. Above this, embedded in the wall was a ruby crystal. So, if you have ever watched Relic Hunter on the idiot box, the logical thing to do was push on it. It worked on television, so why not here! They did so and the great stone rolled away to reveal another corridor. The children being curious, as children are, proceeded through the second tunnel till they came upon another room. This room was quite different from the first. On entering, they walked on a pale blue ceramic floor with a large glass pyramid in the center. Ornate silver sconces lined the walls. In this realm, light was everywhere, so flashlights were not required. On stepping closer to the pyramid, the front opened and created an entrance to a unique world, of which the children had never seen. As each child entered, they were transported, as if in an instant, to an unknown realm. When all was said and done, they stood in a place that seemed like a room but not a room. Large portraits hung on walls that were not there. They walked on a floor that didn't exist. It was as if standing still in the midst of time. But this time warp had no limits.

One portrait seemed to draw their attention more so than any other. It was larger than the others taking up most of the imaginary wall. When gazing upon it, one could see a beautiful young woman with long silky blonde hair. She sat on a throne of soft-petalled pink, white, and yellow roses. This throne stood in the middle of a picturesque meadow. At the foot of her throne was a doorway in the hollow of a great tree. The woman's deep blue eyes drew them closer when gazed upon. As the children came closer, the door beneath her throne opened and, as if in a trance, our crew stepped into the portrait one by one. Unknowingly they had let destiny of the surreal take over.

I must enlighten you on the woman in the picture. It will have a great bearing on our story. For, without her, we would have no story. So, you see how important she is! The woman in the portrait was Rapunzel. When she had let down her hair so that Rumplestiltskin could climb up, her evil stepmother had been watching. She didn't have much use for Rapunzel, or her boyfriend. This stepmother wasn't the nicest of people. She had a bit of a mean streak in her. Being jealous of Rapunzel's beauty, she banished her to the portrait – the one on the invisible wall. I told you this wasn't ordinary! Since that time, Rapunzel had been waiting through time for someone to rescue her and get her out of this mess.

The children found themselves in the meadow where Rapunzel now resided – temporary she hoped. How temporary? We're not sure as of yet. But we can't just leave the poor girl in this situation, can we? After informal introductions, the children sat in a circle surrounding Rapunzel and listened to her forlorn story. Being compassionate children, they knew they had to help poor Rapunzel get back to her rightful place in time – back to her fairy tale where she belonged. But how to do this? This is where Rapunzel was a big help. Somewhere in the meadow lived a Cheshire cat named Puss n' Boots. He held the key that would save her from this dismal fate. They must find him. Puss n' Boots would lead them to a place where the golden scissors were kept. To break the spell the evil stepmother had placed upon her, Rapunzel must cut off her beautiful long hair. But it could only be done with the golden scissors. She could keep it stylish, but it must be cut. On hearing this, the children went on the hunt for the elusive Puss n' Boots. They would spread out and work in pairs. Along their way, One and Two ran into Peter Rabbits' nephew Floppy. He had been given this name due to his ears. Floppy was a lop-eared rabbit. He had moved here before the Internet came into being so he missed the download rules. If you've read chapter three, you know what I'm talking about. Floppy hadn't seen Puss n' Boots in quite a while, so he wasn't sure of his whereabouts. He told them they should ask Pokey the groundhog. Pokey might be of some help. He didn't live far from here.

Meanwhile, Three and Four who had gone in another direction ran into the polka dot giraffe, Elmer. His job in the meadow was to oversee the goings on here and report back to Rapunzel. This was the perfect occupation for someone of his stature. But, to their dismay, even Elmer hadn't seen Puss n' Boots lately. Elmer directed them to the home of Simple Simon. He may be able to give them some insight to their problem. So, on they went to Simon's house.

Five and Six met up with Rocky Raccoon. He was your local busybody. If anyone knew anything of Puss n' Boots' whereabouts, surely Rocky would. As always, onto the next house.

Seven and Eight did the same, but in another area of the meadow. They stumbled upon Old King Cole. He was a bit of a grouch, but harmless. He knew nothing either. Old King Cole sent them onto Foxy's home. He lived at the edge of the meadow. If Foxy didn't know, he could ask his friends in the underground community.

Nine and Ten had headed towards Bullwinkle's residence. He lived in the deeper forested area. Even he could not help them.

Eleven and Twelve were directed to the stream. Maybe Sammy Salmon could shed some light on the subject. So, off they went. On reaching the stream, the children noticed Froggy sitting on a rock taking in some rays. They asked him where they might find Sammy Salmon. Froggy informed them that he lived just a little ways down. You couldn't miss his house. Just look for the flag with a Pisces sign. Sammy was a bit of a patriot when it came to water creatures. Twelve took the lead and followed the stone pathway along the stream till they came to Sammy's domain. Sure enough, there was the flag. Sammy couldn't be far away. Froggy decided to help things along so he would see if he could locate Sammy for them. All the creatures living in the meadow loved Rapunzel and wanted to see her smile again, something she hadn't done in a very long time. Rapunzel had always been kind and sweet to all who lived here, but they knew she didn't really belong. Now, put yourself in her situation. How would you like to be stuck in a picture for eons? See what I mean.

This journey was really starting to frustrate the children. Surely Puss n' Boots must be somewhere! Luckily for them Sammy had heard through the grapevine that Puss had taken a short vacation and was due to return tomorrow. To aid in their search, Sammy called the elusive Puss n' Boots' home and left a message on his answering machine informing him of the existing dilemma. Not to worry about him ignoring this. This cat was adamant when it came to his messages. So the children met up at a previously discussed location to wait for their so desperately needed hero. The grass in the meadow was velvety soft and with no bad weather in the forecast, a night's sleep here would not be so bad. It didn't compare to their pillowtop posturepedic at home, but it would have to do. Jack and Mildred had gone out and purchased them all Sealy Posturepedic mattresses after returning from their visit to Bo Peep. After all, you must support family and besides that, it was an extremely comfortable product. Anyway, back to our tale. All settled in for the night sitting around the campfire, roasting marshmallows and hot dogs.

They were getting kind of hungry. Luckily, Eight and Nine had had the insight to pack a lunch for everyone. While they were waiting for Puss n' Boots to arrive, they discussed how they were going to explain this one when they returned to camp. Even I would like to hear that one!

The next morning, sure enough, Puss n' Boots arrived as scheduled. He had returned on our airline of choice "Chicken Wings Express". The children were elated to see their hero. Puss already had a heads up on the situation, so an explanation was not necessary. He would help them with their task as soon as he put his things away. Unknown to anyone in this story or any other, was that Puss n' Boots was the keeper of the Golden Scissors. This legacy had been passed down in his family for generations. Before him had been Sylvester. You didn't know this, did you? Well, you do now. It's amazing how much data one can learn in a fairy tale. Puss led our crew through the deep-forested area of the meadow not too far from Bullwinkle's house. They had walked right by it earlier but did not know it. There, under the stump beside the twisted tree were the Golden Scissors. They were wrapped in a blue velvet cloth inside a silver box. Puss n' Boots opened the case, just to make sure of things. Everything was still in order. Now they could proceed with their task. The children One through Twelve were truly happy. They could now help their newfound friend smile again. It was too bad she had to cut off that beautiful hair, but they would make sure she had a really upbeat coiffure. All rushed to Rapunzel to tell her the news. Rapunzel was so thrilled she couldn't stop laughing. You see, she had a bit of a nervous disorder, so this is why the laughter. Just for a few minutes though. It subsided after a short time and she came back to reality. You have to realize that sitting in a portrait that long is bound to have some negative effect. Once she returned to her tale, she would make an appointment with her psychiatrist. After a bit of therapy, this disorder should go away. It must have worked. To this day, or until this story, no one knew that she even had any problems – mental or otherwise. No rules existed or were specified as to how she had to have here hair cut as long as it was done with the Golden Scissors. So, in order that she look presentable and in fashion, our crew took Rapunzel to the nearest hair salon in the meadow. It was run by none other than Vidalles Sassoning. Talk about luck or what! He would give her the latest cut so she would be in sync with everyone upon her return. Maybe this hair-cutting thing isn't so bad after all. Just to make it a little more chic, Vidalles gave her a few highlights while he was at it. As you can imagine, she looked like a real fox when he got done with her! Even Rapunzel herself liked it. She should have done this years ago she thought. But then if she had, Rumplestiltskin wouldn't have been in the picture would he? After all was over, it was time to get back to her fairy tale.

Rapunzel and the children returned to the place of entry. Children One through Twelve inclusive said goodbye to their friend and just maybe someday they would see her again in the fairy tale books. They would put in a good word with Mother Goose just to seal the deal. They waited and watched Rapunzel disappear in time until she was no longer. I will tell you more of how she fared out later. The children stepped out of the portrait one by one and found themselves back where they started their journey. Now comes the hard part. They had to get back to their rooms without anyone seeing them or even knowing they had left. Quietly One though Twelve inclusive tiptoed back to the dormitory and into their quarters. Luckily all this had taken place through the night so everyone in the castle was asleep. No one would ever know where they had ventured and the secret of the castle would be preserved through time. It must have been. Have you ever heard this before? If you have, you're one step ahead of me!

Now, I will inform you, because I know you're worried about Rapunzel of how she made out. Well, she was successfully returned to her tale. The evil stepmother was banished to the Tower of London and still resides there as far as I know. When Rumplestiltskin laid eyes on Rapunzel, he was astounded. That haircut really did something for her. She wasn't just beautiful, she was hot! Anyway, to make a long story short, the two were married. Their wedding was an auspicious occasion. Everyone came, even her friends from the meadow. The happy couple had decided to honeymoon in Hawaii. Both Rapunzel and her beloved enjoyed the warmer climates and loved to surf. Actually, Rumplestiltskin had been the local surfing champion 4 time warps running. He had to have a hobby to occupy his time while Rapunzel was away and surfing seemed logical to him. I know you're gonna think surfing! What's with that? On their second date, Rumplestiltskin had taken Rapunzel to the local drive-in to see the latest Frankie and Annette movie. Since then, the two were hooked. So, surfing became the occupation of choice. Afterwards, the happy couple purchased a spacious bungalow; very tastefully done I might add, in Miami, Florida. Neither of them wished to reside directly in the city due to the crime rate and all. But the outskirts suited them just fine. The weather was similar to the islands and they could keep up with their hobby. So now you know what happened to Rapunzel and Rumplestiltskin. I know you're wondering how they managed financially. It turned out quite well for them. The royalties from their fairy tale paid off substantially, so money was never an issue.

Back to the children. Next morning, One through Twelve awoke, a bit sleepy, but none the worse for wear. They dressed and made themselves ready for the day's events. After a hearty breakfast, everyone was directed to the stables. They were to have their first riding lesson. Unicorns are known for their beauty and unknown to most, their temperament. They were the perfect specimens for this task. One, Two and Three would ride the minicorns and the rest would ride the regular unicorns. Five, Seven and Nine rode quite well considering it was their first time on a horse – or somewhat of a horse. They seem to have natural balance. The remainder of the children thought it was ok, but were not totally impressed. They just couldn't seem to get into it. These things happen you know.

Twelve, being a bookworm and a very curious one at that when it came to the supernatural asked permission to skip out on the remainder of the events of the day and go to the library. Since they had such a great time before, this library thing may have a few more goodies up its' sleeve. Twelve's undiscovered genius mind noticed an odd looking box on the shelf just above where he had found the diary and blueprints of Dracula's Haven. He walked over to the box and picked it up. After thoroughly examining the aforementioned cube, he observed strange symbols on each side. Its' lid had an opening. On the underside was a key attached. The object reminded him of a jack in the box. Twelve remembered reading about something of this nature in one of his books back at Southfork. For some reason or another, he couldn't remember where or how he had acquired the book, but knew he had it. Of course, curiosity took over from there. Twelve took the key and opened the box. You won't believe who popped out. Yours truly, Jack in the Occult Box! I told you things weren't going to stay normal. This find really threw

Twelve for a loop. He wasn't sure what to make of it. When Jack greeted him that almost put him over the edge. Now, a Jack in the Occult Box that talked - that's not something you hear of everyday. Jack asked Twelve how his day went and was there anything he would like to know. Twelve eventually calmed down and told Jack to keep his voice low. They were in the library you know. Also, Twelve didn't want anyone to know of his discovery. Jack told his newfound friend that he was a psychic box. What else would he be, being an occult cube? You must have figured that one out! I guess by now, not a whole lot would surprise you in this story, would it? Twelve had a lot of questions for Jack. Like how he came to be a talking box and end up here. You have to admit; an event like this would spark anyone's curiosity. Jack gave Twelve all the necessary explanations. This satisfied Twelve and they went on from there. Now, Jack had a bit of a problem. He was tired of being a Jack in the Occult Box. He wanted to be just a regular Jack in the Box that all the kids loved. Twelve didn't find that to be much of a problem. He would help him with this endeavor. Jack made one request of Twelve. Their association must be kept secret. It was just part of the rules. You've heard of rules, haven't you? If you didn't have them, could you imagine where you would be today? Again, let's not even go there! Surely in one month Twelve could turn Jack around and change his outlook on life as he knew it. The two agreed. Twelve would see him everyday for their "Be a Good Jack in the Box" lesson. Jack had a lot to learn, so, for the times when there were no lessons, Jack was to read the book called "How to be a good Jack in the Box – for dummies". Twelve apologized to Jack for the title. He was no dummy Twelve informed him. It's just the name of the series. Jack thanked Twelve. He had never had a friend before. This was a whole different ball game for Jack and he liked the feeling very much. So, it was settled. Unknowingly to either of them, the pair would become inseparable before Twelve would leave for home.

Twelve returned to join the others. One through Eleven had had a busy day. After their riding lesson, all took a break for a cool glass of tropical lemonade. This camp didn't serve regular stuff. It was imported directly from Jamaica, along with the tasty coconut juice from the Grove. After their break, they had an archery lesson. Guess who was their instructor? Yours truly, Robin Hood. After all he was the best in his field besides stealing from the rich and giving to the poor. Something like our government program except theirs worked. Now, take Robin's way, switch it around and now you know why ours got so screwed up. Do you seriously think the government could actually get anything right? I say no more. Robin had signed a five year contract with the camp. He would take a leave of absence from his fairy tale for two months every year. He decided the change of pace would do him good. It also helped that the children liked him. They thought he dressed a little on the funny side though. No matter, he was a good coach all the way around.

It was getting close to the supper hour. The children were instructed to get cleaned up and make themselves present in the dining hall. When the meal arrived all the children applauded. They were ecstatic to see what was on the table – pizza and soft drinks. I know it's usually pizza and beer, but these are minors after all. We have to keep this story legal. Besides, one hundred inebriated children and bows and arrows so close by could be a little on the dangerous side. Wouldn't that be living on the edge! Too much edge for me thank you! Dessert was the best three layer chocolate cake, besides Mary Poppins', they had ever had. If this was camp food, bring it on!

All the campers were allowed a couple of hours of free time after the evening meal. Twelve snuck away from the others to see how Jack was doing. The rest went to check out the remainder of the grounds they had not seen yet. Sleep would not come easy for them this night. As always, there is someone in the fairy tale world watching over all children. One through Twelve inclusive were no exception. Their sleep guardians were Wynken, Blyncken, and Nod. I don't know if you've ever heard of them, but the trio is well known in the fairy tale realm. After their voyage to the sea of dew, via the river of crystal light, they had retired their wooden shoe. It had been damaged in a storm and was beyond repair. Until another shoe could be built for them, they would be the temporary guardians of sleep for all children. Seemed like the logical thing to do. Besides that, they didn't have much of a choice. This assignment was handed down from the top brass. I guess things are no different no matter where you live.

Next day, a field trip was planned to visit the local tourist attraction, the Village of Cream Puffs. It was a little place on the upland corn prairie many chicken miles from the sunset. Situated all by itself on the big lone prairie where the said destination goes up on a slope. There the winds play around the village. They sing summer songs to it in the bright sunlight and winter ones in its' rightful season. Sometimes, when the wind gets a little too rough, it picks up the tiny village and blows it off away in the sky all by itself. In the center of the town square is the Roundhouse of the Big Spool. When this occurs, the roof is taken off the roundhouse and inside it is found a large spool of heavy thread. This thread is attached to the village. The string winds looser and looser as the wind blows. When things settle down, the people of the village come together and begin winding the spool and bring the village back to its former location. So, when you see a funny looking cloud in the sky, just maybe you're seeing the Village of Cream Puffs. Now, is that a field trip or what!

The children thought this a real blast! They had never seen a village made of cream puffs before. It was quite the sight to see and there was a local bakery there that specialized in guess what? If you haven't figured out it to be cream puffs, you may have some major mental issues that really need solving. If I were you I would definitely check into it. And don't wait. This could be serious.

Since all the children had been very good this day, they were allowed to go to the bakery and sample all the delicious treats there. No one had ever tasted cream puffs so light and airy. After all they must be light if the village could levitate. Everyone took treats back with him or her. No need for Tim Horton here. They may make good coffee, but cream puffs – they couldn't touch these. They were literally out of this world. When the tour of the Village was over, it was time to get back to Dracula's Haven.

What I haven't told you yet was that if the children were to misbehave, a punishment was in order. And it was a goodie! Check this out. All children that needed discipline were not given detention. They were sent to the Town of Liver and Onions. Here, they would have to sit down and have a supper of which this town was famous for – liver and onions. Now, you tell me, what kid wants this fate? It's almost as bad as broccoli and cauliflower. Now, you and I may appreciate a meal of this nature, but a kid – I don't think so! Luckily, this was very seldom necessary. And the ones that realized this fate never went back for seconds. Don't we all wish this worked in real life? We should be so fortunate. Now you see why One through Twelve inclusive did not want to get caught while on their adventures through the secret passages of the castle.

Once back at the camp, all the children retired to their rooms. It had been a busy day. This cream puff thing had taken a lot out of them. Just to grasp the concept was mind-boggling. Imagine being there! As usual, Twelve went to the library to see how his friend Jack was getting on with the book Twelve had given him to read – "How to be a Good Jack in the Box" for dummies. Jack was serious with regards to his endeavor. He greeted Twelve with warmth and sincerity. Twelve was impressed. With a pupil like Jack, this task should be a breeze. It's a good thing that Jack lives in the fairy tale world. A box that talks to you is a bit much for reality. We have enough people that talk to things without adding a box to their problems. Wouldn't the shrinks have a field day with that one!

Things were going pretty smooth at camp. One through Twelve were having a blast. Time seemed to fly by. It wasn't long before the month was almost up. In order to celebrate the first semester, a concert was scheduled. This would be a very special one. Entertainment would be brought in from the outside. It just happened that a traveling show was passing through the area. The coordinators of the presentation had gone and checked it out to make sure it was suitable for children. They were thrilled at what they observed. The main characters in the show were Dahlila the black cow, Bumclock the little brown beetle, a mouse named Petunia and a bee called Buzzy. Buzzy would play the harp, Petunia and Bum-clock would dance an Irish jig. Then, Dahlila, who happened to have an operatic voice like an angel would perform her version of Madame Butterfly. Dahlila had her own rendition of this tune. She knew how to rock it and man could she do her thing! The kids loved it. Her back up was the new group "The Pots and Pans ". All the children had heard of them. And to get a chance to see them in person, what a thrill! Needless to say, the show went off without a hitch. Everyone loved it and the P.R. would benefit the camp to no end. Now things seem to fit the norm so far. But as you know, this will change. You haven't heard a show ending like this one before. When the curtain fell, the old man – we will call him Old Willie Winkie – picked up all the creatures and put them in his pocket. This was their normal way of traveling. This saved them a bundle on flight costs and accommodations. Even Chicken Wings Express couldn't beat that rate. It sure kept their credit card balance down. And with the interest rates on those things being what they are, it's a good thing. It wasn't hard for the troop to be profitable with overheads so low. When it came time to perform again, Old Willie Winkie would take them out of his pocket. At that point all would go back to a reasonable life size form so the show could go on.

Now that we have informed you of how things work in this surreal world, it is time to get back to Jack and Twelve. If you recall, I told you that the two would become inseparable. Twelve didn't want to say good-bye to his friend. Surely there had to be a way the two would not have to part. Twelve would sleep on it. When he awoke the next day, a solution came to him. For this, he must speak to Jack (of the beanstalk) and his mother Mildred. Using his cell phone, he called them and told them of his dilemma. Mildred had seldom refused Twelve anything. As long as he was a good son, there was no problem. And Twelve was a very special boy. His grades were in the top five at school and he was her first born. Now, how could she refuse him? So, Mildred discussed he situation with Jack and he agreed to help in the matter. Money was no object for this family. Jack left Southfork and headed to Dracula's Haven. This should be done face to face - not on the phone. He had called ahead and arranged an appointment with the head honcho of the camp. On arriving, the two went into the office, sat down and proceeded to solve Twelve's problem. Jack agreed to make a generous donation to the camp should Twelve be able to keep his box friend. The head master of the castle was surprised to know that Twelve even knew of Jack in the Occult Box. He also knew that the little box had been very sad for a long time. If this is what Jack in the Occult Box wanted, he would agree to it. Twelve was called in to the office. The three would go to the library and ask Jack (in the box) if he was agreeable to this. When they did so, the little cube was thrilled. At last, a loving home! Who could ask for anything more. The only stipulation was that should anything happen that Jack could no longer live at Southfork for any reason whatsoever, he was to return to Dracula's Haven. A contract was drawn up, adoption papers and all, to keep everything legal and binding for both parties. Twelve was the happiest he had ever been. Twelve helped Jack pack up his belongings, making sure he had everything, including the instruction manual, just in case Twelve got dementia or something. One never knows about these things. Even fairy tales can have flaws. So, one must be prepared. This scenario fits in well with the imagination, but as to the real world, it could create a bit of an issue. You know what they do to people, who talk to boxes, don't you? They take them away and give them a new theme song – "They're coming to take me away, hee hee, ha ha!" I write about boxes but be assured, I don't talk to them and never have, even though you might think it after reading this story.

Since Jack was already at Dracula's Haven, he would stay over and load up all the children One through Twelve inclusive and return to Southfork. The children were happy to return home but a little sad about the whole thing. They had never had such a good time and interesting too! You have to give me credit. No other camp will ever compare to this one. It would turn into the most popular one that ever was in the fairy tale world.

The trip home wasn't as bad as Jack thought it would be. The children were fairly quiet for the majority of the journey. It had been quite the experience for them. Just wait till they tell Quick and Quack of their adventures. This would really blow those chickens minds'. On arriving home, the children unpacked and all went to the pool area for a family barbecue. Afterwards, the children told of all their unusual happenings at Dracula's Haven. Everyone had his or her ears on big time! No one had ever heard of anything like this before. Not that it's out of the norm in this tale or anything. We will call it adventurous. How does that sound? I like it and that's what counts, doesn't it?

It is now time to leave you. I hope you will continue to follow the lives of our fairy tale friends. They sure were happy to meet you! I'm hoping the feeling is mutual. They asked me to tell you to remember that anything in the world of imagination is possible. It must be. If I can write this stuff, you know it's true.

CHAPTER 6

Now it is Cluck and Johephra's turn. A business trip was scheduled for the two of them. A possible new financial venture required their attention immediately. There was a property to be checked out in South America and one in Scotland. I will tell you the reason for this shortly. But for now, knowing they had to go will suffice. Quick and Quack would be at summer chicken camp so the timing was perfect.

Cluck checked her estrogen levels to make sure time was still ticking on her biological mechanisms. She would have to put the purple boxes on hold till they returned. She would bring her purple box pills with her. She must start taking them the day before departure. Cluck didn't want to start popping out purple boxes everywhere. After all, it was a private matter. I know you wouldn't have to carry large amounts of cash with you but don't you think it would get a little embarrassing and just a bit awkward? So, Cluck did what was necessary to put things on hold – only for about one month.

Johephra made all the arrangements necessary for the trip. Reservations were booked early enough through "Chicken Wings Express" – our airline of choice. Their destination was Rio De Janeiro, South America. You see, Little Bo Peep had been keeping in touch. She had too many sheep and was not equipped to handle the younger generation coming up. They were a bit much for her. Mutton 123 had their hands full already.

A decision was made to purchase land in one of two areas. One was in the northern part of South America and the other in the southern part of Scotland. Both areas were prime sheep land, but only one was needed. Whichever one suited them best would be purchased. A training camp for the younger counting sheep was necessary. Cluck and Johephra would fly to South America and check things out. Afterwards, the fine-feathered pair would head for Scotland and survey the situation in that area. After a final tally a decision would be made.

Cluck made sure everything they needed was packed for both. She double-checked her list. She made lists you know. How else could the poor chicken remember it all? And don't leave it up to man. We've all been that route before! Now you know why Cluck did the packing. This packing thing involved a lot of stuff – personal items, day clothes, evening dresses and matching shoes of course. And then she had to get Johephra's gear ready also. You can't really go out dressed to kill without being color coordinated. Wouldn't that make a fashion statement and a half! Could you imagine? The same went for Johephra. All his best suits were sent to the cleaners so they would be pressed and ready at a moment's notice. On checking his shoes, Cluck reminded him that he had to go out and purchase a few new pairs. He had to buy them in pairs. He did have two feet you know. His were getting a little worn, so newer ones, of the latest design were needed. We're talking about the shoes here, not the feet. After all, when you're trying to catch fish don't you use your best lure? No different here. Do you see the similarities? If not, I won't even try to go there. That's more than I can handle at this point in time.

Quick and Quack were delivered to chicken camp at Dracula's Haven with no regret I might add. Children One through Twelve inclusive had given them the heads up on the place, so the pair was pretty excited about going. What the children didn't know, Jack in the Box filled them in on the rest. Jack was no longer an Occult Box. Just thought you might want to know this. I know you were quite concerned about his welfare. Remember those lessons. Well, they paid off in a big way. He was now a stable and well adjusted Jack in the Box. All thanks to Twelve. We had best get back to the task at hand. We are getting away from ourselves. This is not the story to be told here.

Cluck and Johephra flew out the next day to Rio De Janeiro, South America. Their liaison stationed there would meet them at the airport. At that point the pair would go to their hotel to rest up for the meetings and tours scheduled for the following day. Cluck and Johephra were staying at the "Chicken Hilton". This establishment had a five star rating as chickens go. Johephra wanted nothing but the best for his Cluck. As usual, their liaison, Slowly Gonzales, checked on matters in order to ensure that all was up to snuff. And it was of course. You don't think they paid him the big bucks for nothing, do you?

Slowly met them on arrival at S.A. International. (That's South America – by the way). Abbreviations are acceptable in this story. Sometimes you have to make your own rules and this is one of those times.

I know you've heard of Speedy Gonzales, Slowly's famous nephew. The two were similar in a lot of ways, but different in others. Both were small in stature, sharp with quick minds, but their speeds – well, let's just say they were at opposite ends of the spectrum. Slowly was not quick with the forward movement, but he could still keep up. What he lacked in speed he made up in other ways. You know what I mean. I shouldn't have to explain further. I don't feel it necessary at this point in the story. If you haven't gotten the picture by now, you're never going to. I would give up if I were you. Why put yourself through any more misery? Just deal with it is the best advice I can give you. But, I'm not a shrink; so don't take my word as gospel.

After a good night's sleep, Cluck and Johephra dressed (appropriately of course) and took the elevator down to the dining room. A good breakfast is an essential part of the day. At least that's what the two believed. Fast foods weren't really popular in the fairy tale realm. McDonalds hadn't arrived yet! Even imagination has to stay healthy.

The property they were to view this day was a one and a half hour drive, give or take a few chicken miles, from the city. Rio wasn't what it is today – not quite as expanded. The land was owned by Guiseppe Peppino. He had emigrated from Italy years ago, upon inheriting this from some relative. I can't recall which one, but they were related. At least that's what the lawyers told him. The land in question was about as scenic and picturesque as you could get. Lush green pastures for miles at the base of the South American mountain range. The area encompassed five thousand acres, so a tour by helicopter was arranged. Cluck and Johephra couldn't take forever to accomplish their task. Besides, Little "Bo Peep was getting really stressed out over all these extra sheep. The younger generation can do that you know. Put you over the edge!

The residence on the property was quaint but tasteful. A little bungalow with flowers growing all around. Should they acquire this piece of heaven, a new main house would have to be constructed and the bungalow would serve as staff housing. A barn was non-existent so a very large one would have to be built also. One must have a place for the sheep to come in out of the weather and there is always the all- important roll call. So far this seemed perfect for their new venture. When Johephra asked to see the books, Guiseppe escorted him inside their humble abode into his office. There he handed Johephra all the necessary documents for him to review. All was in perfect order. Guiseppe was quite the bookkeeper. He had been a chartered accountant for a major firm in Rome in Italy. But the stress from the job had gotten to be too much for Guiseppe to handle. It was starting to take a toll on his family. So, he sold all his assets and got away from it all. This is why he now resides in South America. Guiseppe was retired now and his children grown up and gone. The place was too much for him at this stage of the game.

The ledgers were all in order. This was a good sign thought Johephra. It took a couple of days longer to finish things up. Actually about four more before the pair would move on to Scotland. Cluck and Johephra took a minor vacation while there. Why not? They were there anyway. Cluck checked out the local markets. She had a thing for doodads – just couldn't stay away from them. Good thing Johephra had put a limit on her credit card. Otherwise he would have to charter a cargo plane to haul all her stuff home. And going through customs! Officials would have a field day or a major headache.

Their flight left at 10:00 A.M. that morning. "Chicken Wings Express" was right on schedule as usual. They would arrive in Scotland the following morning. This was due to the time difference. You may not have realized, but giant chickens get jet lag too. No wonder Cluck and Johephra felt so tired on arrival. The climate here was a little cooler than South America. Good thing Cluck packed a few heavier things to wear – just in case. You have to admit she sure knew how to look after Johephra. He knew it too. Maybe that was why he doted on her so much. We all wish! I better quit there before I have the entire male population up in arms. And that's not the intent here. Enough with the comments. Let's move on.

Their host Diablo McPhee met the feathered pair at the airport. He was surprised to see how large they were. I don't think anyone informed him that they were of the giant species. Was he surprised! Good thing he didn't show up with a Volkswagen Beetle. Trying to cram two giant chickens into one of those could be a little on the tricky side. Luckily for Cluck and Johephra Diablo had brought the limo. Due to the location of the property, Diablo had arranged for the visitors to stay at the local bed and breakfast. There were no five star hotels here. Have you ever seen one in rural suburbia? If you happened to find one, let me know and I will pass the word on. I think Cluck and Johephra might be interested. I can't guarantee that, but you never know. Actually, the out of the way tourist trap – in the middle of nowhere – turned out to be very inviting with large comfortable rooms. With handmade quilts on the beds, matching curtains, and a fireplace in every room, this inn had a quaint cottage orientated air about it. It was as if it just walked out of a fairy tale. Cluck and Johephra felt right at home here. It reminded Cluck of her humble beginnings, when she was just a giant baby chick. This was before Bartholomu had captured her. She had been happy there. Not as happy as she was with Johephra of course. She hadn't met him yet, so how could she be. Enough with the mush, we shall go on. The elated couple would take a day to rest up – jet lag and all. It does take a toll on a person or chicken, whichever the case may be.

I know you're wondering, what's with the name? This is what happened. His mother's name was Diabella. She originated from Brazil. While on a student exchange program to Scotland she met George McPhee. They fell in love and were married one year later. George was refused an international visa, due to some political conflict between the two countries. Diabella, coming from the upper echelons of her society, and with much political influence, had no problem with this issue. For them to be together, Diabella left her native land and moved to Scotland to be with the man she loved. Her family thought highly of George, so they pushed the issue. And you already know the results of that. Besides, they didn't want to see Diabella end up an old spinster. When Diabella bore her first child, so as not to offend the relatives on either side, she and George agreed upon the name Diablo. This satisfied both sides, they thought. It does sound kind of cool! Don't you agree? A few locals raised their eyebrows on this one, but they would have to learn to adjust. They should look at the brighter picture. They didn't name the kid Methuselah or something weird.

Breakfast had been arranged to be served at 10:00 a.m. They had to sleep in sometime in this tale. Why not now? It fits doesn't it? The cook, Miss Muffet of Glencove, prepared a traditional brunch for them. Scones, homemade jams, and black pudding. Johephra found their menu to be a bit odd, but they were in a different country. And not all cultures have the same taste in food. Not everything is done the American way. Both found the meal delicious, except for one item. The black pudding, (and it's not chocolate) they weren't quite sure about. Cluck tried it, but found it wasn't to her liking. I don't think Cluck should have done that. And you'll know why in a minute. Not twenty minutes later, her feathers started to fall out. Johephra was o.k. He hadn't tasted the pudding. Cluck found out the hard way that she had an allergy to it. She didn't go bald or anything like that, but she did end up with a few embarrassing patches. Something must be available somewhere to fix the problem. Chicken surgery was out of the question. Johephra went to see the innkeeper. Maybe there was someone in this local who could help. Johephra didn't want Cluck to have a feather breakdown. That would not be healthy for a giant chicken – or anyone for that matter. The woman at the front desk, Wanda Feather-bed, did know of someone. With a name like that she must have some data on the subject. Wanda made a call through Zucchini Telecom (our communication system of choice) and set up an appointment for Cluck. I told you that telephone company was international. Do you believe me now? Johephra would keep an eye on things for Wanda while she escorted Cluck to see the local witch doctor, Ethel. A conventional medical practitioner is of no use to a giant chicken, especially one that can lay purple boxes. Only a healer associated with the realm could help Cluck. That's just the way things are in this part of the imagination. Having a bad hair day is one thing, but losing your feathers, that's serious stuff. Wanda had informed Ethel of the problem via e-mail. We do a lot of that in this story. This way, Ethel would be fully prepared on her patients' arrival. When Ethel saw Cluck, only then did she realize the severity of the situation. She quickly checked her book "The Witch Doctor's Manual of Best Recipes". To her dismay, the very page she needed had been torn and part of the required ingredients were missing. What to do? Ethel thought for a moment. She was a quick thinker so it didn't take her very long. She would get in touch with her colleague the Purple People Eater "Chartruse". She had been with her when she graduated to the witch doctor's union. She had a copy of the book. Chartruse had helped Ethel in her study group for the final exams, which Ethel had passed with honours. She had even made the Dean's List. I have heard of a witch making the list, but never a witch doctor, and of the surreal world at that. After getting her degree, Ethel had opened a small practice in the area. The locals, being a superstitious group, kept Ethel busy enough to make a decent living despite her overheads. It also helped that the government insurance here covered witch doctor calls. You have to admit; at least here no one had to mortgage their house should they require medical attention. Maybe one should take a lesson from these guys. They seem to be in better shape than we are.

Chartruse agreed to see Cluck. Wanda called Johephra on her cell – there were no pay phones in the area. Zucchini Telecom had not expanded to that level here. Since everyone here had cell phones it didn't seem financially feasible to invest in a public phone system. Johephra was relieved to hear the news. Wanda would keep him posted as to their progress. Wanda and Cluck took a taxi to Chartruse's office. It wasn't a large place. There wasn't much call for a purple people eater these days. Not since the Internet had come into being. Chartruse was a minute fellow with the oddest of hair. His name said it all. Yes, he was of the male gender. Anything after that, you figure it out. His attire was something to be desired, but then, what else would you expect. With a name like Chartruse and pink hair, it isn't hard to see why. Now that you have the lowdown on this strange little fellow, we can proceed to fixing our problem, Cluck.

Chartruse opened the "Book". Sure enough, he had the solution to Cluck's feather issue right there in black and white. He told them to have a seat, make themselves comfortable (as much as you could when you're losing your feathers) and he would return in about twenty minutes with a potion that would fix her right up. True to his word, Chartruse returned with a small bottle of purple liquid. What other colour would he have? He was a purple people eater, not blue, green, yellow or any other colour. Cluck wasn't quite sure about all this, but upon informing her there were no adverse side effects, she downed the contents of the bottle in one gulp. Even though she was a giant chicken, this stuff was pretty potent, so a large dose was unnecessary. In an instant Cluck's feathers returned – no more bald patches. She was one happy chicken let me tell you. Cluck paid the fee for services rendered by Chartruse, with a major tip on top of it, and both were on their way. Cluck promised Chartruse she would never eat black pudding again. She had learned her lesson – the hard way at that. To this day, Cluck avoids black pudding like the plague. She also would make sure that it didn't happen to anyone else. She would post it on her website on her return home. This fate should not befall any other chicken in the future. Not everyone could afford to fly to Scotland to see a purple people eater. Johephra was ecstatic on hearing the news. The pair could now go one with the task at hand.

The following day Diablo directed them to the designated property. The terrain was a little on the rough side, but sheep, especially this breed, are very adaptable creatures. So, the landscape was not an issue. During winter months the sheep would need appropriate attire. All those custom made parkas would be very costly. Sheep and parkas don't exactly go together. And how would they learn to be counted when their numbers were covered by heavy winter gear. Even though the property was less expensive, the overheads would eat up too much of the profits. Johephra got in touch with the powers that be in Southfork. It was decided to pick up the deal in South America. Cluck and Johephra thanked their host for his time and effort. Diablo was disappointed in their decision but understood their reasoning. He would do the same if he were in their shoes.

As instructed Cluck and Johephra flew back home to Southfork to commence the required steps for the purchase in South America. The lawyers were to draw up all the necessary papers. No problem there. This was the easy part. Now comes the fun part. Visas had to be acquired for the junior counting sheep involved. The lambs would not go. They were too young. Only the teenagers were to be shipped out and as quickly as possible. Bo Peep was starting to lose it! Have you ever tried to expedite matters when dealing with govern-

ment agencies? Talk about a dilemma! It's a good thing
the family had connections in the right places. It took
about one week to cut through the red tape, but finally
all the paper work was in order and the project could
proceed as planned.

Jack flew down to South America to oversee the construction of the new structures necessary. It didn't take
long. The "Quick Construction Company" was true
to it's name. They guaranteed Jack everything would
be up to par with all the building codes. And it was.
An ironclad warranty went with the job. Quick Construction Company had never once had to return and
redo a job. They were the best there was in the area.
Their references were impeccable. Don't worry, Jack
was known for doing his homework, so he knew all this
before hiring them.

Back in Australia Little Bo Peep had to make ready
all the sheep. They would be issued temporary letters
for now. You see, numbers were only assigned on graduating counting sheep school. Bo Peep was sent all the
necessary documents through "Chicken International
Express. If it sounds familiar, you're right. "Chicken
International Express" was an affiliate of "Chicken
Wings Express". Something like Air Canada but a little
more on the efficient side. This was a lot of sheep to
move, so "Chicken Wings Express" brought the big
guns in on this one – their supersonic "Chicken Wings
747". It was equipped to handle sheep, giant chickens, just about anything. Since seating on these crafts

accommodated one thousand passengers, all first class I'll have you know, five of them would be required. This way, all the sheep could be relocated at the same time. Cheaper than flying back and forth. And the time it would save. The old saying time is money definitely applies here. And could you imagine dealing with five thousand sheep, all having jet lag at different times. I agree with Jack. He really did make the right choice here.

As scheduled, the entire younger generation of these four - legged creatures were loaded up, told to fasten their seat belts, and off they went. The airline had a very good supply of motion sickness medication - just in case. You never know till it happens and one should not wait to the last minute, especially for this. Let's leave that alone. It could get a little messy if you know what I mean. As it turned out the trip went off without a hitch. Surprising in this story, isn't it! Other than a bit of jet lag, all arrived safe and sound. Upon reaching S.A. International, the sheep were transported to their new training camp. Everything had been made ready for their arrival. As they came off their mode of transpor-tation, the sheep were instructed to go directly to the main building. Here they would receive their temporary letters. The drill instructor gave a short demonstration of how to place the letters – with precision naturally. Afterwards, they were assigned rooms, given a tour of the premises, and told to be at the dining hall at 5:00 p.m. for the evening meal. I know sheep don't usually follow this protocol, but these were special sheep. The majority were literate and to the staff's dismay, very computer save! This will cause a problem, but I will tell you about that later. For now, getting everyone settled in was enough, believe me. You just try and accustom 5000 sheep – all with jet lag. See what I mean.

Now, there was one sheep out of all of them that had a slight problem. There's always one in the crowd that has to be different. But no one knew he had a sight issue. I will give you some insight into this so you will see where I'm coming from. Since the sheep had to abide by the roll call rules, when one is out of order, it is noticed. They had hired Digit McPhee. And you know from before he was the best. Digit observed that this one lone sheep was never in the right place during roll call. He had reprimanded him over and over again, but to no avail. This sheep was either not too bright or had a problem. So, Digit sent him to the infirmary for a complete physical. He wanted to rule out any medical reason. At least this way they would know for certain what the problem would or would not be. His blood work came back normal, his x-rays were fine – no brain tumors or anything like that. Upon giving him an eye exam, it was discovered this sheep had latent dyslexia. It had gone unnoticed in the past. Back home, his best buddy was named Bob. He just followed Bob's lead and things went on smoothly. But now, Bob wasn't here. This sheep was on his own. Not knowing he was dys-lexic, the sheep in question was not sent to the special school required to correct this. Now it was too late. They would have to come up with another solution.

I know I told you all the sheep would have letters till graduation day, but due to the nature of the problem, the number 44 seemed an appropriate solution. Of course, the number would have to be written on a small scale. This sheep, we'll call him Mickey, would be issued a large number 44 upon graduating to the mutton union. Just maybe, if Mickey worked really hard he would pass with honours. Mickey really wanted this. He would show the others who sometimes made fun of him that he was as smart, if not more so, than they were. Also, the sheep with the highest mark would receive a scholarship. It was designed to help the students take care of their union dues. To be a counting sheep was quite an honour. But like anything else, it didn't come for nothing. Upon graduating, all counting sheep must join the mutton union. And as you know unions like the almighty dollar. Nothing new there, is there? But at least here, subsidies were available. No one was left out. Now you see why Mickey was such a driven sheep. He wanted to be the first sheep with latent dyslexia to graduate the top of this class and make imagination history.

I told you all these sheep were computer save. All time in the computer room had to be monitored. But we are talking about the younger generation. As you know, from personal experience, they don't always do as told. No different here. Some of these sheep had a bit of a twisted mind. Not when it came to doing their job, but in other areas – like the sights on the Internet where young sheep should not go. You guessed it, the sheep porn sights. The staff had no idea that these sheep knew as much as they did when it came to the computer. They were about to find out. Every instance the sheep were given free time in the computer room, one or two of the pc's would crash. Someone would have to come in and straighten things out, reload all the programs, and set things right. After a while, this was getting to be a bit of a nuisance. The monitor was present during their free time, so they didn't associate the problem with the sheep. Sheep can be pretty discreet when they want to – especially when involved in something that is off limits. Just to be sure of things, the head of the camp ordered blocks put on all the unsavory sights. That should solve the problem. And it did till a new one came along.

The majority of the sheep were well behaved. They followed the rules, and did what was necessary to be good student sheep and not end up at the sheep corrections facility. But, (there's always a but in this story) as in anything else, there are a few bad apples in every bunch. Nothing noticeable to say, but they were there. Remember I told you these sheep were quite computer save. Some of them knew even more than their instructors. This new generation of sheep was a pretty sharp crew. Three sheep in particular stand out from the rest. They enjoyed living on the edge of discipline. You know the kind – very headstrong, but borderline genius in certain fields. And this field happened to be technology. We will call them Eeny, Meany, and Moe. I know these names are a bit strange for sheep, but it was the first thing that came to mind. So, they will just have to do. The three always hung out together whenever possible. They were, as one would say, computers geeks. Neither of them looked geeky. Have you ever seen a geeky sheep? See what I mean.

Now, Eeny, he was a whiz at programming. Meany was your system configuration specialist, and Moe was especially apt at hacking. Isn't that a deadly combination! Bill Gates would have loved these three. But these four-legged muttons lived in the imagination realm, not reality. So, Gates couldn't have hired them even if he wanted to. Could you just picture that? Sheep and people doing pc work side by side, and the sheep outdoing them. Wouldn't that be a sight to see! Maybe it's not so far fetched. I have observed animals that are a lot smarter than some people I know. I think it time to quit there. I wouldn't want to alienate the few friends I do have. And by the way, this statement is not directed at them. I want to make that point perfectly clear! Eeny, Meany, and Moe had devised a plan to use the computer room when no one was around. They had been thorough in their research. Our trio knew the timetable down to the minute. One night, after all had retired for the evening, our inquisitive creatures found their way to the computer science lab, turned on the pcs, and started. I know you're thinking they wanted to get into the porn sheep sights, but you're wrong. Neither of them were those kind of sheep. They were not rams as of yet! You see, teenage sheep hormones kick in later than ours. And I won't take that any farther. Something had come over the news station earlier in the day that had caught their interest. They just had to check this out. Since the information had leaked out over the airways - without consent – it intrigued them. They were just that kind of sheep. Having the knowledge they did, it wasn't long before they were bringing up classified government information. Meany had tapped into the mainframe of the chicken government computer system. By the way, when it came to breaking codes, these sheep were crackerjacks! The scary part of the whole thing is that they understood this stuff – more than some of our government employees that do this for a living. If this makes you nervous, it should! They were getting deep into the system when a security warning came up on the screen. Eeny, Meany, and Moe thought it best if they shut down for now. Our trio would return and delve further into this mystery at a later date – like the following night.

The following night, as planned, Eeny, Meany and Moe returned. They went straight into where they had left off. As our trio dug deeper, they found themselves in the chicken archives. These archives held the secrets of the feathered community in the fairy tale domain. Here was buried the legend of the purple boxes and how they came to be. Only Cluck and Johephra knew of this. This data was not designed for public knowledge. The repercussions would be disastrous should the secret get out. The Great Creator (remember her –from chapter 4) of the realm of imagination had foreseen this and so this is why the secret was buried deep in the archives long ago. It was meant to be found by no one, let alone a crew of nosy sheep! Unknown to them, a curse or virus – it doesn't matter which- one is as bad as the other – would befall those who delved into the sacred chicken archives without the written consent of the Great Creator. Written consent keeps things legal, just in case it ended up in court. And we want to stay legal in this tale. We're twisted enough, we don't need the law on our tail! Our band of hackers was not of the superstitious nature, so they shrugged off the warning that had come up on the screen before they opened the document. Having an off beat sense of humour, they laughed about the whole thing. Really, purple boxes! That was absolutely ridiculous! No one believed in this mumbo jumbo anymore, not even in the fairy tale world. Little did they know!!! They decided to keep this fiction (as they called it) to themselves. Besides, if anyone found out they were in the computer lab after hours and without permission, Eeny, Meany, and Moe would be in hot water big time! The sheep corrections facility didn't really appeal to them. It was late, so our crew shut down for the night and proceeded to their assigned quarters.

Next day all seemed fine. It wasn't till a few days later than events started to occur to make our little group rethink this curse thing. The weather had been bright and sunny, so neither of them thought anything of it when their wool began to change colour. They just thought they had gotten a bit of sunburn. As each day went on, the colour started changing to a pale blue. A week later, you couldn't miss them. Three indigo sheep walking around is pretty obvious don't you think? The school, being concerned, sent them to the infirmary. The staff there didn't know what to make of this. They had never encountered blue sheep before this day. It was decided these sheep would be sent to the nearest sheep trauma center. They were specialists in the sheep department there. And, after all, blue sheep is pretty serious stuff. Surely they could find a solution to this really bad hair day! On arriving at the center, the staff was shocked at what they saw. Never in a million years – and that's a lot of them in the imagination realm – had anyone ever seen such blue sheep. They tried everything they could think of, even to the point of bleaching their coats, but to no avail. It started to look like this blue might be permanent. Little did they know that only the imagination world could help them? In order to receive this help, the three in question had to come clean on what they had done. If they ended up in the corrections facility so be it. At least you can get out of there at one point in time. But to be blue through all eternity, that's something no sane sheep wants. If they were birds, there wouldn't be a problem. But they weren't. All three proceeded back to the school and straight to the head mistress. Her name was Dorothy and yes, she did have red shoes. And no she's not the same one. Maybe a distant cousin, but not the one with the dog named Toto. After disclosing what the three had done, Dorothy sat them down and explained what was necessary for the colour reversal to begin. Being the big cheese here, Dorothy knew exactly what to do and who to contact. So, here we go again. Bring in the spooks to fix the problem.

As usual, an e-mail was quickly dispatched to none other than the world re-known colour expert, Oriole of Paris. She had performed miracles or what seemed like it on hair that even the top hairdressers wouldn't touch. Follicle transformation was her specialty. Now, when it comes to sheep, well, we'll see what she can do with this one. Everyone in the fairy tale world knew what she could do with pink flamingos. Did you know they used to be white at one time? A pink flamingo was unheard of. White was the only colour they came in. Only when Oriole discovered the secret of their true genetic colour did they become so popular and pink! This popularity even expanded beyond the fairy tale realm. Their demand become so great it was unbelievable. An executive secretary had to be hired just to keep up with bookings in their social calendar. The birthday season was an especially busy time for them. Even the secretary had her hands full keeping up with appointments. It got so bad a three- month waiting period was the norm. So, I'm telling you now, if you require the attendance of any of these pink flamingos, you had better book well in advance or you'll be out of luck. Enough with the birds, let's get back to the task at hand.

We left Eeny, Meany, and Moe very blue and forlorn. Only until they heard the famous Oriole was coming in for the job, did a glimmer of hope come into their eyes. She must be able to do something for these poor creatures. To face a future of being blue and sad (because of it) would stress anyone out. And that could be a very, very long time in the fairy tale time warp. Not a very good outlook, is it? Oriole knew this, so she packed up her best bag of tricks from her inventory and flew via our favourite airline of choice in this story, "Chicken Wings Express" to her required destination. I thought that was pretty good of her, being so famous and all. Let's be real here, she didn't need the money or the prestige. Oriole was of the most compassionate and understanding nature. Now, there's a switch for you – someone rich and famous and still real. Or as real as it gets in this tale! Not something you see every day.

On arrival, Oriole was brought straight to the quarantine room where our three blues brothers were being kept. Just to be on the safe side, Eeny, Meany, and Moe had been quarantined. No chances were being taken, just in case this blue thing was contagious. Do you realize that if this was and it had gotten away from them, blue would be the only available colour in sweaters? And can you imagine if blue was not your colour. Talk about a fashion faux pas! See how disastrous the repercussions could be on this one. This was a major that absolutely had to be fixed. Oriole took one look at them and being the expert she was, knew what had to be done. She had to reverse the colour process. Opening her acclaimed hair book (everyone has one in this story-a book that is) she found the blue sheep recipe. The italics on the bottom of the page had the instructions for the reversal process. Actually, it was fairly simple. All the ingredients had a special combining order. Oriole had to reverse the order of entry when creating the potion. So, in the antiseptic lab that had been created for her, she went to work. It wasn't long before Oriole had everything ready. Eeny, being the oldest, was first. Then came Meany, then Moe. After each had downed the potion, they fell asleep one by one. The reversal process would take four hours. This wasn't any old dye job you know. The colour had to change from the inside out. Four hours passed. All three awoke and headed for, you guessed it, the nearest full length mirror. One after the other, they checked themselves from head to toe (didn't want any patches you know). You've never seen such wide smiles on three sheep in all your life. Oriole inspected them and was very pleased with the results. She could put another notch in her belt for this one. Luckily for them, and because they were so good at computer tech, neither of them ended up in the sheep corrections facility. Believe me, our three culprits learned their lesson, and very well I might add. Being blue (and it was definitely not their colour) was enough punishment for anyone!

As for the file that got them into this mess, it was removed from the computer and is still impossible to access to this very day. It remains under strict security buried deep in the "Chicken Archives".

Now that the crisis was over things could get back to normal. All the sheep were doing extremely well in their counting studies. They would make excellent models for the future generation of counting sheep to be. The school's future looked very optimistic.

Now that all the sheep disasters were out of the way, everyone could get back to business as usual. Eeny, Meany, and Moe made Dorothy a solemn promise to keep on the straight and narrow. The remainder of the herd made a pact that they would be exemplary sheep. Of course, the sheep corrections facility may have had something to do with their decision. Dorothy had reminded them that a mark on their record could come back and bite them down the road. A clear record was a pre-requisite for graduating to a full-fledged counting sheep. This really hit home with them. Can you blame them? Have you ever tried to get a job (and not washing dishes) with a police record? These sheep may be curious but they are definitely not stupid!

The remainder of the year went fairly smooth. The odd crisis here and there, but nothing serious. Our sheep worked very hard and it wasn't long before the end was near. Graduation Day was quickly approaching. Excitement was in the air. It wouldn't be long before they were legitimate posturepedic counting sheep. Now, that's something to be excited about! I know if I were a sheep, I'd be hyped about the whole thing. But, I'm not a four legged fuzzy. If I were, you wouldn't be reading this story. I know these sheep are special, but writing a book! That's a bit much even for me! Let's leave them alone and let them do whatever it is that counting sheep do in their spare time. I know they like to play on the telephone. I've seen them do it and actually, so have you at least once a week. Enough with playtime. Back to graduation.

The eventful day finally arrived. The caps and gowns were there, the caterers had prepared a marvelous buffet, minus leg of lamb of course. That would just be rude! We won't go there. Little Bo Peep flew over for the auspicious occasion. After all, these were her future employees. Bo Peep was surprised at the polite mannerism of the entire herd. She would be honoured to have these sheep at Mutton 123. Boot camp had turned out to be a huge success. Jack, Mildred, Cluck, Johephra, Daisy, Toronado, Ophillia and Bernard had also come via our favourite airline in this tale "Chicken Wings Express". It was their investment after all. And you won't believe who showed up to hand out the diplomas. None other than yours truly, Snydley Bedtime, the president and c.e.o. of the Sealy Posturepedic Company. All the important people in the mattress industry were there.

When the certificates were handed out, our sheep got the shock of their wooly lives. Remember I told you that number 44 wanted to be at the top of his class. Well he did! He had passed with honours – even made the dean's list! Pretty good for a sheep with latent dyslexia, don't you think. 44 was so proud. No one would laugh or make fun of him any longer. When he gave his acceptance speech he did it with so much class you'd never know he was mildly literally challenged. I don't know about you, but I think he earned it. He had busted his butt to get here. 44's future was solid now. He wouldn't end up on the unemployment line or taking a temporary job as a speed limit sign. Not this kid!

Now that all are members of the mutton union, we can close this chapter. Sleep will come a lot easier for you now, knowing our counting sheep are all safe and sound in their fairy tale world. Hope all is well with you as is with our over the top counting sheep. See you in chapter 7.

CHAPTER 7

Since our last chapter things have changed a little. Jack and Mildred are still at Southfork. They'll probably be there forever, or until this story ends, whichever comes first. I must say the last time I saw them, the couple seemed quite happy together. The children One through Twelve inclusive are away at school now. Both Jack and Mildred had decided that since they both lived in a fairy tale world, the ordinary schools would not suffice. So, after doing some research and if you know Jack he was quite thorough on this issue, a decision was made to send their offspring to one of the best institutions in the fairy tale realm – "The Magical School of Higher Learning". Here, they would be taught the necessary skills to be successful in their time period. It happened to be located on Fairy Island. This fit right in. Queen Fiona and King Alberto could keep an eye on things for Jack and Mildred. Ever since their visit, they had kept in touch with each other. Talk about things working out all the way around.

Just so you know, Mildred gave up on children – having them that is. I think she made a wise choice. Twelve is more than enough for anyone. Can you blame her? I'd like to see you take on that many kids on a permanent basis and not end up in the psychiatric ward at your local loony toone factory. Anyway, it all panned out well for everyone.

Daisy and Toronado are still together. They have a large herd now. Toronado had gone into the cattle business, as you know. Let's face it, this was right up his alley. Both Daisy and Toronado were quite thick in the cattle barons association. And well liked too! So much so that Toronado was voted president for two years running. He still acts as consultant to this day. Daisy fit in like a glove in their social circles. As you know, she loved all the parties. But that wasn't all she was good at. She became head of the charity for over the hill bovine. This way, none would end up you know where? Surely I don't have to mention that word in this tale. It just wouldn't be right.

Bernard and Ophillia are still together and living at Southfork. I know they didn't have much of an adventure in this tale, but Ophillia had more than her share of encounters before she met Bernard. Since marrying Bernard, she had settled down a lot. Suzie home-maker she'll never be, but surprising to everyone she had become quite the homebody. She was truly happy with Bernard. Richard Geere he was not but what he lacked in looks he made up in other ways. And anything after that belongs in the adult section of the bookstore. Surely you can figure this one out. If I have to explain further, I suggest you make an appointment with Dr. Ruth. Maybe she can help you. I sure hope so, for your sake!

Quick and Quack finished high school and were accepted into the Julienne Academy of Arts for Giant Chickens. It was an exclusive school with the highest of ratings. Both chicks were naturals when it came to drama. They ended up graduating with honours and are presently negotiating a contract with a major television studio for a new series "The Chickens of New York". By the sounds of it, it should be a hit. I sure hope so. They worked really hard for this. If I were you I'd watch for them in the upcoming new shows in the spring lineup for next season. I know you wish them all the luck and so do I. It's about time chickens got a break. After what we do to them, we owe them that much. I say no more!

Unfortunately for her, Cluck met up with something called menopause. You know how it goes. The hot flashes, the mood swings, the whole works. If you don't, consider yourself lucky. Believe me, I know! It was really getting out of hand, so she decided (with Johephra's full support) it was time for a visit to the local veterinarian. I don't have to tell you what happened there. Let's just say menopause and the purple boxes were no longer an issue when she left the office after her day surgery. Chickens are not like us. They recover a lot quicker than we do – really quick! Now, Cluck and Johephra could get on with their lives and Johephra wouldn't end up in the world of prozaic. Now, isn't that a happy ending! Don't we all wish life were like that in the real world. Maybe this realm of imagination isn't so bad after all.

By the way, our crew needn't worry about finances. There had been enough purple boxes to last twenty lifetimes. And the financial investments made by the powers that be at Southfork had paid off in a big way if you know what I mean.

Now that you've read this final chapter, you can put your Nytol or whatever you use to get some sleep away. Your stress will disappear and you'll be back to normal knowing that all our characters are doing well in this twisted fairy tale.

The moral of this story – there is none. Just the twisted imagination of a creative writer.

THE END

NOTES FROM THE AUTHOR

In everyone there is an imagination. What we do with it is up to us. We can ignore it or create a world beyond our own. I feel that this world should make us laugh. Laughter is a great remedy. A smile can welcome anyone we encounter in this place we call life.

If I have put a smile on your face or made you laugh then I have accomplished my goal. With this I leave you and maybe we shall meet again in my next book!

About the Author

D. A. STEWART was born and raised in the community of Blind River in Northern Ontario, Canada. She attended Blind River High School and went on to complete her education at Ottawa University in Ottawa, Canada. She has resided in the small town of Desbarats for the past fifteen years and still does today.

D. A. Stewart possesses an uncanny ability to communicate with the animals in her life. Her cats, dogs, horses, and bird all seem to know what she is thinking and vice-versa. She is an accomplished riding instructor in all aspects of the equine arts.

She is an energetic lady full of life, ready to accept any challenge that may come her way.

Gardening is one of her passions, with a green thumb to go along with it.

Whether you find her at her computer, building fences or re-modeling her house, she is doing it with gusto. Her husband likes to refer to this as: "Watch out! Denise is on a mission".

To know her is to appreciate her sense of humor, her ability to focus, her boundless energy, and last but not least the twisted mind that wrote this story.

Printed in the United States
45228LVS00001B